Teenage Bluez II

Published by
Life Changing Books
P.O. Box 423
Brandywine, MD 20613
www.teenagebluez.lifechangingbooks.net

Life Changing Books and the portrayal of a person reading are trademarks of Life Changing Books.

ISBN: 0-9741394-8-3

Library of Congress CIP: 2005929424

Printed in Canada

Acknowledgements

The authors of Teenage Bluez would like to give thanks to God for guiding our hands and thoughts to write these stories. Prayerfully, these stories will help teenagers from all over the world who are experiencing similar situations.

We would also like to thank our parents, who gave us the encouragement when we needed it the most. To our friends, you all know who you are, we say thank you!

To the technical support, Kevin Carr, thanks for designing such an eye catching cover. Thanks to the book cover model, Jamica. Kathleen Jackson, our Project Coordinator, thanks for all of your help and work.

TEENAGE
BLUEZ
SERIES 2

Table of Contents

HER SECRET
by Marketa Salley

"You finish ya homework yet?" Kia's mother, Gwen asked, as she walked by the kitchen table.

"Almost," Kia said, flipping through her notebook.

Everything was going well until Kia's stepfather, James, chimed in. "You woulda' been finished if you hadn't been on the phone with that boy all day. You're only fourteen!"

Kia sighed and closed her notebook. "So much for finishin' now," she mumbled.

Kia and her stepfather going at each other was an everyday occurrence. She blamed James for her mother and father not getting back together. Gwen never told Kia that it was her father's consistent infidelity that had kept them apart.

Four years earlier, while out with friends at a concert at Constitution Hall, Gwen spotted James at the concession stand, sipping on a beer. He was 6'4, and a bit on the heavy side, so she looked away, not wanting to be bothered. But after taking another look, she thought James was kind of cute in his black double-breasted suit and brim hat. She decided to let him know she was interested, so she gave him a slight grin. Getting the message, James walked over and introduced himself like a gentleman. After a short conversation, the two exchanged numbers.

Two months later, Gwen invited James to Kia's tenth

birthday party to introduce him to her friends and Kia. As soon as Kia laid eyes on James, she hated him. She expressed her dislike of James to her mother, in hopes that she would stop seeing him. But Gwen was so happy, she ignored her daughter's obvious attempts to get James out the picture. Instead, a year later, he moved in with them.

James felt the pressure Kia was putting on Gwen to put him out, so he decided to put a stop to it. He whisked Gwen down to the justice of the peace and married her a few days after Kia's twelfth birthday. Although she wasn't able to convince her mother not to marry James, Kia vowed never to let her guard down around him. There was something dark and dangerous in his eyes. She would have never imagined in a million years that one day her instincts would prove to be true.

Gwen and James fondling each other in the kitchen made Kia sick to her stomach. Unable to contain her disgust, she let out a heavy sigh.

"Isn't it time for you to go to bed?" Gwen asked, with an attitude.

"Since when do I have a bedtime?" Kia asked, picking up her books and walking down the narrow hallway to her room.

"You betta watch your mouth young lady, or you'll find yourself in this house for the rest of the week!" Gwen yelled.

After quickly changing into her pajamas, Kia got into bed. Under the covers, with the lights out, she clutched her pillow tightly and imagined it was her boyfriend, Andre.

Kia had been dating Andre for two months. She had met him at a neighborhood party. He was her first real boyfriend, and nothing like the boys in her Southeast Washington, D.C. neighborhood. He was 6'3, built like a basketball player, and an honor roll student at a private school across town in the District. To a casual observer, Andre was just another kid from the hood, but that was far from being true. In fact, he was rich — *filthy rich*. You wouldn't know it though. He was down to earth and didn't seem to mind that Kia's family was broke as a joke.

* * *

Friday morning, Kia leaped out of bed the minute the alarm went off. She showered and quickly dressed in her Apple Bottom Jeans, a screen tee that read, *Future Actress*, and her favorite silver necklace. Her short hair, cocoa-colored skin, 5'6 thin frame, and flair for the dramatic, made her a shoo-in for Hollywood.

Although her junior high school graduation was two months away, it seemed to be taking forever, and the boys seemed to be more annoying than ever. One day, they decided to play stupid games, like who could burp the loudest, or who could make the loudest bodily noises in class. Kia thought they acted like they were in kindergarten instead of junior high. Kia's best friend, Whitney, on the other hand, thought they were hilarious.

Whitney and Kia had been friends since kindergarten. People often wondered how they stayed friends so long, since they were total opposites. Kia was very serious, while Whitney was the total opposite. She too was an honor roll student, but unlike Kia, who would have to rely on scholarships for college, was set because both her parents had successful careers. Even though her parents lived in the same section of the city, Whitney lived with her mother in a nice townhouse. Her mother was Puerto Rican, and her father was black, which explained her long wavy hair, bronze colored skin and hazel eyes.

Whitney's mother was a bookkeeper, and her father, who lived in the suburbs, was a police officer for Prince George's County. They had divorced years ago, but remained good friends. Whitney had the best of both worlds. During the week, she would stay with her mother, and on the weekends, she'd stay with her father, who would treat her to shopping sprees at Pentagon City Mall.

As the school day went on, Kia found herself daydreaming more and more about Andre. Her English teacher even caught her off guard by asking her a question in front of the whole class.

"Kia, can you tell the class what is a prepositional phrase?" the teacher asked.

"Umm...umm...it's a...a," Kia said stuttering.

When she didn't know the answer, her classmates laughed. Embarrassed, she slouched down in her chair and rested her head in her hand. *Laugh all you want, it ain't like I ain't know the answer. I just didn't hear the question,* she thought to herself. Kia closed her English textbook, then looked down at her watch. *Yes, time to go.* It was what she had been waiting for all day.

"Girl, let's go to the Rec Center and watch the guys play ball," Whitney said, as they made their way through the front doors of the school.

"Nah, you go 'head, I have to get home," Kia said, running to the Metro Station.

Going to the Rec Center was the last thing Kia had on her mind. She wanted to get home to call Andre. Their daily ritual was school, followed by talking on the phone for hours.

Her ride home was less than desirable. The usual twenty-minute ride, turned into two hours of discomfort because of a delay on the blue line. *Why would they work on the tracks during the middle of rush hour?* she asked herself.

By the time she got home, she knew she had missed Andre's call. She quickly picked up the phone and dialed his cell phone number. To her surprise, he answered.

"Hey, boo. Where you at?" she asked Andre.

"I'm at the Rec Center. Where were you at earlier? I called

you when I got home from school," Andre said.

"They're working on the blue line, so the trains were seriously delayed."

"Why you not up here with yo girl, Whit?"

"I would've came down there if I'd known you were gonna be there. Anyway, how was your day?" Kia asked. "I hope it was better than mine."

"It was a'ight," Andre responded. "But what happened with you today?"

"Well, I was kinda daydreamin' in my English class. My teacher caught me and put me on blast in front of everyone."

"I know that feelin', my teachers put me on blast everyday," Andre said laughing. They chatted a little more before hanging up, but not before giving each other a smooch over the phone.

Later, Kia sat down on the couch and started thinking about how exciting high school was going to be next year. She was snapped out of her daze when the phone rang. It was Whitney.

"Girl, you missed it. Sharee and her crew were all over Andre. I think it's because they know he got paper," she said, exaggerating the situation just a bit to get a rise out of Kia.

Sharee and her crew were well known in the neighborhood for making out with all the boys, especially if they had money.

Kia fell for the bait and started to give Whitney the third degree. "What did Andre do?"

"Girl, he was laughin' and eatin' it up," Whitney said.

Kia almost came through the phone. "What? He didn't tell them to get out his face?"

"Nope," Whitney said, making matters worse.

"You know what, I don't even care. We're solid and there's nothin' those girls can do to change that. But trust me, he'll be dealt with for not tellin' them to step off," Kia said, before hanging up the phone.

Half an hour later, Kia's mom came home in good spirits.

She was so happy, that she walked through the door singing the theme from the *Jeffersons*.

"Guess what?" Gwen said to Kia, who was sitting on the couch watching television.

"What?" Kia asked, surprised that her mom was so happy.

"I'm up for a management position at work."

"Mom, that's great," Kia said, jumping up and hugging her. "Does it pay more money?"

"Yup, and I get benefits too. I can't tell you how happy I'll be if I get it."

Gwen's excitement was short lived. James walked in the house minutes later, only to find dinner wasn't ready. Pissed, he threw his keys across the living room at Gwen, missing her by inches. He looked at her like he wanted to smack the taste out of her mouth.

"Why are you sittin' on your butt, and I don't smell anything cooking?" he yelled.

"Honey, it'll only take me a minute to whip up somethin'," Gwen said, trying to calm him down.

He picked up a magazine off the coffee table and threw it at the back of Gwen's head as she headed into the kitchen. James was right on her heels. Kia got up off the couch and followed them into the kitchen.

"Whip up somethin'? I want a real meal, not somethin' you gon' throw together!" he yelled, smacking her across the face and down onto the kitchen floor.

Kia ran to her mother's side. "Ma, you a'ight?" she asked.

"Yeah, baby, I'm okay. He's just a little upset. I shoulda' been here sooner," Gwen said, in James' defense.

"Stop protecting him! Kick him out!" Then Kia pointed at James and said, "I knew you were trouble the first day I laid eyes on you!"

"What? What did you say?" James became enraged. "Don't

you know she'll kick you out before she kicks me out," he said, grabbing Kia by her hair.

Kia started screaming at the top of her lungs. "Let her go!" Gwen said, kicking him hard in the leg.

Pissed that Gwen fought back, James smacked her across the face again, this time drawing blood. "If you ever hit me again, you're gonna regret it! You hear me!" he said, standing over her. He gave Gwen and his stepdaughter a deadly look, grabbed a bottle of soda out the refrigerator, opened it and started to gulp it down.

Kia helped her mother to her feet then ran over to the drawer and grabbed a knife. Catching James off guard, she pushed him up against the counter and pointed the knife at him.

"Touch my mother again, and I'll slice your fingers off," she said, with venom in her voice.

James saw the rage in Kia's eyes and knew she meant what she said. Defeated, he retreated to their bedroom. Kia and Gwen went into Kia's room, locked the door, and laid on Kia's bed. Rubbing her mother's back, Kia tried to comfort her. *She didn't kick his butt out like I wanted her to, but at least this time we stood up to him*, Kia thought to herself.

* * *

Finally it was June 1st, Graduation Day, and Kia was beaming from ear to ear. She had worked hard and it paid off. Not only was she going to be in the Honors Program at the School Without Walls, she was number one in her class.

"Mom, are you almost ready?" she asked, hustling down the hallway of their two-bedroom apartment.

Her mother laughed. "Kia, we have to wait for James. He's moving like an old man today for some reason."

When Kia heard the knock at the door, she ran and opened

it. Whitney was standing on the other side, with a big grin on her face.

"You ready? My mom is waiting outside," Whitney said, walking into the apartment.

"Yeah, I'm just waitin' for my mom," Kia said, picking up her fake Louis Vuitton purse. "I can't wait to get up outta this camp after high school, cause James gets on my last nerve."

"Y'all still goin' at it?" Whitney asked, plopping down on the couch.

"Yeah, but I'm not gonna let him get to me today. I'm happy and I'm not 'bout to let him spoil it for me."

Minutes later, Gwen and James emerged from their bedroom. Going to Kia's graduation was the last thing James wanted to do, and he didn't hide his feelings about it. He let it be known that he was angry, by constantly rolling his eyes and uttering bad words under his breath.

"Ooohhh! Whitney, you look so beautiful," Gwen said, hugging her.

"Thanks Mrs. Tibbs. So do you."

"Okay, ladies, enough talking, let's get you two down to the school," Gwen said with excitement. They all walked out the apartment.

When they pulled up in front of Jefferson Junior High School, Kia and Whitney touched up their makeup and hair one last time, before running into the school. After finding their places in line, they gave each other a wink and laughed.

In the hallway of the school, Andre met up with Gwen and James. Tension filled the air when the two men laid eyes on one another. Even though they had only met once, it hadn't been a pleasant meeting. James thought Andre was a showoff. Not to mention he felt Andre called the house too much.

Trying to defuse the possibility of a nasty scene, Gwen leaned over to James and whispered in his ear, "Try to be nice.

This is a big day for Kia." She led him to their seats in the auditorium.

James plopped down in his seat, turned to Gwen and said, "Don't you ever disrespect me like that again. You hear me?"

"Yeah, baby, I hear you. But I just didn't want you two to get into it," she said rubbing his hand, trying to keep him calm.

"Don't worry 'bout me. You better worry 'bout him," James said, snatching his hand away.

As the standard graduation song, Pomp and Circumstance played, the graduates marched blissfully down the aisles. When Gwen saw how happy her daughter was she started crying. She had dropped out when she was in the eleventh grade because she'd gotten pregnant with Kia. And since she didn't have a high school diploma, it was hard for her to get a decent job. She worked at a local department store for minimum wage. James, who dropped out in the tenth grade, worked as a maintenance man for an apartment complex. After they paid the bills, there was nothing left over.

That was another reason James hated Andre. He was jealous of the fact that Andre drove a Benz at seventeen, and was always showering Kia and Gwen with expensive gifts. Something he wished he could do.

The parents, faculty and students listened attentively as the Deputy Mayor of D.C. spoke of what awaited the students in the future.

"Life is what you make it. You can be a follower or you can be a leader. Never allow the negativity of others keep you from achieving your goals. Remember, middle school may be over, but your education continues. From here you go to high school, then off to college," the man said to the crowd of more than two hundred.

After the Deputy Mayor's speech, the graduates were presented with their diplomas. As Kia strolled across the stage, her mother snapped shots of her with a disposable camera she had bought from Target. Kia was glowing, and it was at that moment Gwen noticed she was no longer her little girl, but a young woman.

After the ceremony, Kia ran over and showed her mother and Andre her diploma. She totally ignored James, like he wasn't even there.

"You did good baby," her mother said, embracing her.

Andre smiled. "I'm proud of you, Kia," he said, hugging her tightly. "By the way, why don't you and some of your friends come by my place for an after graduation party?"

"Can I, Mom?" Kia said pleadingly.

"I guess," Gwen said, looking at James for approval. James said nothing. He didn't even congratulate Kia. Instead, he walked outside and lit a cigarette.

"Yes!" Kia said, hugging her mother.

"Alright. I'll see you guys later. Make sure y'all bring your swim gear, cause we have a huge outdoor pool," Andre said.

Later that night, Kia and her friends all met up at Andre's house in Bowie, Maryland to celebrate.

"Are you sure your parents won't mind?" Kia asked Andre, once she and her friends arrived at his house.

"No, they're out of town. They're always out of town," he said, as if he almost missed them.

Andre was used to his parents always being on the go. His father was the CEO of a computer company, and his mother was a gynecologist, who was also the Director of Obstetrics at George Washington Hospital. Andre had been raised by nannies, so he didn't know what it meant to grow up in a home with loving and attentive parents. That had been all right when he was young, but as he grew older, he would do dumb things to get their attention. Of course, it never worked, and that frustrated him. It was like he was invisible, and half the time, they would forget they even had a child.

This was Kia's first time at Andre's, and she felt like she was in heaven. His house was a castle compared to the two-bedroom apartment she shared with her mother and James. Standing in the driveway, Kia admired the gigantic house. She looked through the multi-pane windows and was taken away by the fabulous family room.

"C'mon, let's go in," Andre said.

The kids walked in and were greeted by the housekeeper, Mrs. Martinez.

"Dang, Andre, man. Y'all got a maid," one of the kids said.

"No maid, Senore', housekeeper! Housekeeper!" Mrs. Martinez said, offended. "Now come. Come." She led the bunch through the French doors, into the recreation room that had a pre-wired 5.1 surround sound, a cozy wood burning fireplace, and a custom wet bar.

"There's a top of the line security system installed, so don't anybody think about takin' home any party favors," Andre laughed.

Once they had changed into their swim gear, the group made their way out to the in-ground swimming pool with Jacuzzi. As they splashed around in the pool, Andre motioned for Kia to come inside with him.

"Where we goin'?" Kia asked, walking in the house behind him.

"To my room," Andre said, running up the stairs.

"Andre, I don't think we should be in your room when your parents aren't here," she said, standing at the bottom of the stairs.

"Why not? My parents are cool with me having friends in my room."

"Are you sure?" she asked.

"Yeah. Now come on up."

Reluctantly, Kia followed Andre up to his room. When she entered, she couldn't believe her eyes. His room was bigger than her whole apartment. The first thing that caught her eye was the beautiful, king size brass bed. She walked into the adjoining bathroom, and had to catch her breath. It was bodacious, with a whirlpool tub surrounded by windows, a separate shower and double sinks.

Sitting on the bed, Andre patted the silk black comforter. "Kia, come sit with me."

She walked slowly over to the bed and sat down. She knew what he had on his mind, and it scared her. Once she sat down, he gently massaged her leg and kissed the side of her face. Then he tried to slide his tongue into her mouth.

"Andre, remember what we agreed on," Kia said, removing his hand from her leg. She slid away from him.

"I know, but I want you," he said, pulling her back towards him.

"I think we should wait. We don't have protection. Besides I'm not ready for this," Kia said, as he tried to unzip her jeans. "Andre, I never told you this, but I'm still a virgin."

"That's cool. I'll guide you through this."

Kia knew she couldn't let something happen between them. She knew too many girls who had gotten pregnant while they were still in junior high.

"Andre, I don't want to end up like some of the girls my age in my neighborhood. They're walkin' around pushing baby strollers, or chasing after their kids in the grocery store. You see it everywhere. They've had to give up their teenage years for one night of pleasure."

"Don't worry, nothin' will happen," he said, still trying to get in her pants.

"You don't know that. It only takes one time." Kia moved away from Andre again. "Do you know the girl upstairs from me is fourteen and pregnant? Her mother is mad at her and her boyfriend left her."

"I would never do somethin' like that to you."

Kia knew that line all too well. Most of the girls she knew said their boyfriends told them the same thing until they got pregnant. Then it was, "It ain't mine, or I ain't ready to be nobody daddy."

She saw the effects having a baby had on their lives up close and personal. When her friends who had babies would show other girls pictures of their babies, they would say, "Ooohhh, she or he is so cute. I wish I had one." All she would think is, *are these girls crazy*?

It wasn't just about dressing them in cute clothes and showing them off. There were day-to-day responsibilities involved in taking care of a baby, and that was hard when the majority of them were still kids themselves. Their education suffered, and most of them just dropped out of school and ended up on welfare. Bottom line — she didn't want to become a statistic.

Andre let everything Kia say go in one ear and out the other. "Kia, come on. It's gonna be alright."

"I can't," she said trembling.

"You can't or you won't? You know there are plenty of girls who'd love to be with me, but I chose you. Now you want to front on me. Forget it," he said, jumping off the bed.

Instead of following her instincts, Kia fell prey to his reverse psychology and allowed him to undress her. Inexperienced and scared out of her wits, she laid there while Andre took full advantage of her vulnerability. When he was done, Andre rolled over on his side. He looked at Kia and noticed she was crying.

"What's wrong?" he asked, not understanding why she was crying.

Wiping her face, she said, "Nothin'."

Frustrated with her behavior, Andre got up and showered. By the time he returned to his bedroom, Kia was gone. Sure that she was outside, he got dressed and walked out to the pool.

"Where's Kia?" Andre asked Whitney.

"I don't know. I thought she was with you."

"She was, but after I got out the shower she was gone."

"She left with Khandi," another teenager said, sipping on his soda.

"What? Why did she leave?" Andre asked confused.

Whitney pulled Andre to the side. "Why were you in the shower?" She raised her eyebrows and said, "What y'all do?"

Not wanting to answer the question, Andre left and went back inside. The moment he stepped in the house, his cell phone rang.

"Yeah," Andre said, after seeing Kia's number on his caller ID.

"Sorry I left so abruptly."

"Well, why did you leave?"

Kia tried to find the right words to express what she was feeling. "I think we should cool it for a while. I can see that you want to take our relationship to the next level and I'm not ready for that."

"I understand that, but let's talk about this."

"Andre, I just need some time."

Although that was the last thing Andre wanted, he agreed.

For days afterwards, Kia wouldn't accept any calls from anyone, including Whitney. She was scared out of her mind that she and Andre had made the biggest mistake of their lives. *How could I have had unprotected sex with Andre? What if I'm pregnant?*

Aggravated by Kia's strange behavior, Whitney went over to her house. When she rang the doorbell, she could hear Kia's stepfather and mother yelling at one another.

"Hey, Whit, how you doin'?" Kia's mother asked, opening the door. Trying to hide the bruises on her face, she quickly turned away from Whitney.

"I'm doin' fine. How 'bout you, Mrs. Tibbs?" Whitney said.

"I'm okay," she said, barely making eye contact with her. "Kia's in her room."

Whitney strolled down the hall to Kia's room and opened the door. "I know you ain't tryna avoid me," she said, walking into the room.

"No, I'm actually tryna avoid everyone," Kia said, sitting up in her bed.

When it became apparent something was wrong, Whitney became concerned and started to grill Kia. "Is James still beatin' on ya mom?" she asked.

"Yeah," Kia said, shaking her head.

"Dang. Why does she stay with him?" Whitney asked curiously.

"I think she's scared to leave him."

"Well, I say we jump his butt," Whitney said, swinging her arms. "Anyway, why haven't you called me since graduation?"

"I've been goin' through a rough patch since Andre and I decided to take a break," she said sadly. "We haven't talked in days. He's called a couple times, but I didn't talk to him."

"Why did you guys break up anyway? What happened at the party?" Whitney asked, lying across the bed.

"Can we please not talk about this?" Kia said, rolling her eyes.

"Okay, I promise not to bring it up again, if you promise to snap out of it. It's the beginning of the summer, and we should be enjoying it. I have to go, but let's hang out this weekend," Whitney said, on her way out.

Teenage Bluez II

* * *

It was ten o'clock on a very warm night in July, with no breeze coming through the window. Kia turned on her fan and sipped her Kool-Aid. Lying across her bed in her daisy dukes and tank top, she wondered what Andre was doing. It had been a month since the two had talked and she was missing him. She was regretting her decision that they spend some time apart, and decided that she would call him the next day and tell him how she felt.

The sound of her door opening made her sit up. She knew it wasn't her mother, cause Gwen had called earlier to tell her that she was working late, and wouldn't be home until after eleven. Walking in, the visitor's tall body towered over Kia.

"What are you doin' in here?" she asked, with fear in her voice. The figure had on a t-shirt and boxers, and his gut was hanging out.

The familiar face said nothing. Instead, he walked over to her bed. Kia crawled to the far end of her bed. She wrapped her hands around her knees and screamed, "Get out! My mom will be home soon!"

Kia tried to grab her cell phone off the nightstand, but the stranger was too quick. He grabbed it and threw it across the room, shattering it.

"Once my mom finds out 'bout this, you're gonna be sorry!" Kia screamed, trying to threaten the stranger into leaving her room.

Ignoring her threats, he threw her back on the bed so hard that it caused her to gasp for air. Tugging at her shorts until they were down pass her knees, he put his right hand over Kia's mouth and whispered in her ear, "Shut up. Scream again and you'll regret it."

"Aaahhh!" Kia grunted in pain.

"Didn't I just tell you to shut up," he whispered, with the smell of alcohol on his breath.

Kia could barely breathe, let alone scream. The fact that he weighed at least a hundred pounds more than she did, didn't keep her from trying to fight him off of her. She started throwing punches his way, and clamped her legs shut, hoping to keep him from doing the unthinkable to her. She even tried to grab the lamp off her nightstand, which was only a few inches away from her head. That didn't work, because he grabbed her arms before she could get to it. Kia felt helpless, as the stranger had his way with her.

After it was all over, the man left, but not before threatening Kia that if she told anyone, he would do serious harm to her mother and her. She knew the memory of this awful night would become her enemy. She was hurt, scared, confused, but most of all, angry. Her next thought was to go to the police. *But would they even believe me? I know he'll just lie and say I made it up.*

For three days, she felt so ashamed she wouldn't leave her room. The thought of anyone finding out what happened nearly sent her over the edge. She tried to bury it, but it was like trying to breathe under water. She was constantly having nightmares of that dreadful night, which often had her contemplating suicide.

* * *

Kia spent her days and nights locked in her room. When her mother would try to talk to her about why she was so depressed, she would shut her out. Gwen was sure something was seriously wrong with her. She eventually called on Whitney for help, who rushed right over. When she arrived, Gwen asked her to come into the kitchen so they could talk in private.

"Whitney, I'm really worried. Kia isn't acting like herself.

She's violent, withdrawn, and severely depressed. Did you two get into a fight or something?" Gwen asked.

"No, ma'am," Whitney replied. Kia crept up on the two of them talking. "Let me talk to her," Whitney whispered.

"Talk to me about what?" Kia asked, plopping down in a chair.

"Kia, what's goin' on? Your mom is worried about you. She said you've been actin' strange, and you've cut yourself off from everyone."

Kia sat in silence, then said, "Look, nothin' is wrong. I can't have a bad day?"

"It's been more like a bad week, if you ask me. Now what's wrong? Did Andre do somethin'?" Whitney asked.

"What makes you think someone did somethin' to me?" Kia got very defensive, snapped at her friend, and threw her out. As she walked down the slender hallway to her room, she bumped into James, who gave a deadly stare that almost made her heart stop.

"What's wrong with the princess?" he said to Kia. She broke down crying and ran to her room.

Needing help with her friend's erotic behavior, Whitney told her mother about the situation and asked for advice.

"Baby, all I can tell you is to talk to Kia. Try to get her to confide in you," she said.

"What if she won't talk to me?"

"Well, you just have to keep trying. Eventually she'll open up. You have to give her time," Whitney's mother said, giving her daughter a hug. "If she doesn't, at least you can say you tried."

Whitney took her mother's advice, and waited a few days before confronting Kia again. On her way to Kia's apartment, she spotted Kia standing on the corner of her street in a daze. As soon as Kia saw Whitney, she started walking in the opposite direction.

"Kia, Kia, wait!" Whitney yelled, running up to her.

Kia turned around and yelled, "Whitney, will you leave me alone!"

"Why are you so angry at me? I'm just tryna help you."

"I don't need your help!" Kia pushed Whitney away.

Whitney didn't let Kia's actions stop her from trying to comfort her. Kia had always been a fun loving person, who was always happy. She loved school and spending time with her friends. So when Whitney saw how upset she was, it confirmed her suspicions that something bad had happened to her.

"I can't believe you're actin' like this. I consider you a sister, and you're actin' like I'm nobody," Whitney said, with tears in her eyes.

Kia sat down on the edge of the curb. The look on her face said it all. She was depressed and terribly distraught about something.

"Kia, why have you been actin' so crazy lately? Talk to me. I thought we were best friends," Whitney said.

"I don't want to talk 'bout it."

"A'ight, let me know when you feel like talkin', because I'm not lettin' this go. We've been friends too long for me to turn my back on you now."

Hearing the concern in Whitney's voice made Kia want to spill her guts, but she couldn't. *What if she didn't understand? What if she thought she had initiated the encounter?* Kia thought to herself. She couldn't deal with the fact that her friend could possibly think she was responsible for what happened, so she kept silent. She felt trapped. She desperately needed to get this burden off her chest, but was too afraid. But she did promise Whitney she would start spending time with her again. They hugged, made up, and headed to Popeye's at the end of the block.

"Hey, you know my birthday is Saturday, right? My dad is givin' me a party at Dave and Buster's downtown. Why don't you come? It'll be fun," Whitney said, eating her chicken and mumbo sauce.

"Yeah, I know. And sure, anything to make up for the way I've been actin'."

* * *

On Saturday, the day of Whitney's party, it was twelve in the afternoon and Kia was still in the bed.

"Get up sleepyhead," Gwen said, pulling back the sheet. "Aren't you going to Whit's party?"

"Yeah, but I don't feel up to it," Kia said, holding her stomach.

"What's wrong?"

"I don't know. I feel really queasy." Kia tried to get out of bed, but couldn't. An hour later, she finally got up. *What's wrong with me?* She thought. *I must be comin' down with somethin'.*

Noticing that she only had an hour to get ready, she quickly took a shower and got dressed. She replaced her Betty Boop pajamas with a pair of Rocawear jeans and a t-shirt. Minutes later, the phone rang. After the fourth ring, Kia stuck her head out her bedroom door.

"Ma, get the phone!" she yelled. When the phone kept ringing, she figured her mother couldn't hear it because she was running water in the kitchen. She ran into the living room. "Hello," she said, picking up the phone.

"We're downstairs," Whitney said.

"I'll be down in a minute." Kia grabbed her purse, kissed her mother goodbye and ran out the door. She greeted her friend with a birthday hug.

"I'm so glad you're comin'. It wouldn't be my birthday without you," Whitney said.

"Hey, what am I, chopped liver?" Whitney's mother said. The girls laughed.

Heading downtown, the girls sang Usher's, *Confessions*. Halfway into the song, Kia became ill. She began to sweat profusely and gasped for air. When Whitney saw her friend struggling to breath, she yelled for her mother to pull over. She quickly pulled onto the median and leaned over the driver's seat to check on Kia.

"Oh, my God!" Whitney's mother screamed, once she saw how pale Kia looked.

"Ma, quick, take her to the hospital!" Whitney yelled, as she jumped in the back seat with Kia.

Her mother made an illegal U-turn, and raced downtown to George Washington Hospital, driving at speeds of up to 80 mph. She picked up her cell phone and dialed 911.

"911 dispatch. What's your emergency?" the operator said calmly.

"My name is Brandy Alexander, and I have a sick girl in my car."

"Where are you now?" the operator asked.

"We're about five minutes from George Washington Hospital. Can you let them know we're on our way?"

"Yes, ma'am, I can, but I need you to stay on the phone with me," the operator said.

Ms. Alexander wouldn't hear of it. She hung up the phone so she could concentrate on driving. Flying through red lights, five minutes later, she skidded in front of the emergency room entrance. Her mind was so frayed, she hadn't noticed that a police officer had been trying to pull her over for blocks. Running to the passenger's side, she was met by the officer.

"Ma'am, I need you to get back in your car!" the officer

yelled, furious she hadn't stopped previously.

"Look, I have a sick child in my car. If you're gonna give me a ticket, you're gonna have to do it later," she said, brushing pass the officer.

The officer said nothing. Instead, he helped them get Kia inside and onto a stretcher.

Whitney and her mom were a wreck. They tried several times to get in touch with Kia's mom, but no one answered the phone.

"Ma, do you think Kia's alright?" Whitney asked in tears, while they were waiting to hear about her condition.

"Sweetie, they're gonna take good care of Kia."

"What's wrong with her?"

"Whit, I wish I knew. But as soon as they know something, they'll come out and tell us," Ms. Alexander said, hugging her daughter tightly.

While Kia was being examined, she noticed the doctor's last name — Benson. When the doctor was finished, she told Kia she'd be right back.

"Excuse me doctor, before you leave, can I ask you a question?" Kia said, sitting up in the hospital bed.

"Sure."

"Ummm, my friend has the same last name as yours, and I just remembered he told me his mother works here."

"What's your friend's name?"

"Andre."

"Well, what a coincidence. That's my son's name too." Dr. Benson laughed. "Now that I think of it, he has a picture of you on his dresser. If my memory serves me correctly, I think you two were seeing each other about two months ago.

"Yes, but things didn't work out."

"I know, he told me. But I can tell you he really thought a lot of you though. I'll be right back." Dr. Benson, dressed in blue scrubs, exited the triage room. She went into the waiting area, where the receptionist pointed out Whitney and her mother.

"Hi, I'm Doctor Cheryl Benson. Are you Kia's mother?" she asked.

"No, I'm Brandy Alexander, a friend of the family. And this is my daughter, Whitney. Dr. Benson, what's wrong with Kia?"

"I'm not sure yet, but we're running tests." She then went on to explain she could only disclose the results of the tests to Kia's parents or legal guardian. "Well, I better go and try to get in touch with her mother now," Dr. Benson said. "Why don't you and your daughter go to the cafeteria and get something to eat. By the time you get back, hopefully I'll have reached Kia's mother."

Dr. Benson walked back into the room where Kia was. Just as she was about to sit down beside her, a nurse walked in and handed her a piece of paper.

"Are those the results of my tests? Does it say what's wrong with me?" Kia asked, with a frightened look on her face.

Dr. Benson didn't answer, but the widening of her eyes and her jaw dropping, was evidence the news wasn't good.

"Kia, when was your last period?" Dr. Benson asked.

"Last month, I think. Why?"

"Kia, we ran some tests and one of them was a pregnancy test," Dr. Benson said, as she sat down beside her. "And the test was positive."

Kia was so full of emotions, starting with disbelief, then fear. Her worst nightmare had just come true.

So many thoughts ran through Dr. Benson's mind as Kia sat dumbfounded. *What if Andre is the father? Will he drop out of school? What if he isn't the father? How will he react to the news?* Although Dr. Benson knew it wasn't a good time to ask questions, she did.

"Kia, who is the father?" she asked.

"It's Andre's. I can't believe you just asked me that. I never cheated on Andre when we were together. Besides, I've only had sex once, and that was with Andre."

Kia didn't realize it, but she had just lied. She had suppressed that night in July so deep down inside, that she considered her night with Andre the only time she'd ever had sex.

As a mother, Dr. Benson was on the brink of losing it, but she had to remember she was a professional at work. She tried to reassure Kia that everything was going to work out. But deep down inside, she knew things were spiraling downhill and fast.

"Do you want me to tell Andre, or do you want to tell him? And Kia, what about your parents?" Dr. Benson asked. Kia started to cry. "I tell you what, you talk to your mother and I'll tell Andre."

"Oh, my God, my mother is gonna kill me!" Kia cried, realizing the severity of the situation.

Her mother's raft was at the top of the list of things she was going to have to face. And with James in the picture, it was going to be even worse. She knew the first thing he was going to try and do was convince Gwen to kick her out. And with her mother's inability to make decisions on her own, she was afraid she would do just that.

Dr. Benson wasn't able to contact Kia's mother, so she released her to Whitney's mother. Kia, Whitney, and her mom left and headed to Kia's apartment. In the meantime, Dr. Benson headed home to tell Andre the news.

* * *

Mrs. Benson pulled her Range Rover into the garage, and sat thinking how she was going to break the news to her son and husband. Feeling she could no longer avoid what was sure to be an unpleasant scene, she went into the house and placed her briefcase on the floor. She walked down the long hallway leading to the library, where her son and husband were playing chess.

"Hey, Ma. How was your day?" Andre said, smiling at his mother.

"I've had better," she said, sitting on their leather ottoman.

"What's wrong, honey?" Ray, Andre's father asked, hearing the strain in her voice.

As hard as it was, she told Andre and her husband about Kia's pregnancy. To say her husband was mad was an understatement.

"I can't believe what a mess you've gotten yourself into!" Andre's father yelled.

"Dad…"

"Shut up!" he said, cutting him off.

"Dad, I'm sorry."

"Didn't I tell you to shut up?" Andre started balling. "Ain't this nothing, a baby about to have a baby," Ray said. "It's too late to start crying now."

Cheryl wanted to console her son, but couldn't. She was very disappointed in him and felt his lapse in judgment may have cost him everything. Andre's parents were having a difficult time digesting the situation.

"So, what does her parents have to say about this? Who are her parents? As a matter of fact, I've never met this girl. Who is she?" Ray asked Cheryl, all at once.

"Well, I just met her today. As for her parents, I don't know. I wasn't able to get in touch with them. Kia said she was going to tell them when she got home." Cheryl let out a heavy sigh. "I'm quite sure they're going to be just as upset as we are."

"Well, what do you suggest we do?" Ray asked. "Andre's

too young to be a father. He's only seventeen."

"Honey, I think we should wait and see what happens with Kia's parents. Then we'll just have to take it from there." Mrs. Benson was exhausted, so Ray told her to go to bed and he'd take care of everything.

"I hope you're happy. You put your mother through hell today and for what?" his father said, chastising him.

"Dad, I made a mistake. I'm sorry," Andre said.

"Sorry ain't gonna cut it this time." The two sat in silence. "Do you realize what people are going to think when they find out about this?" Ray asked. "We're outstanding citizens in this community, but that's all gone, now that our seventeen year old son has gotten somebody knocked up."

"Is that all you can think about? So what if people talk. I thought you'd be more concerned about what I'm going through," Andre cried.

"What you're going through? What about what your mother and I are going through?" he said, on the verge of slapping Andre across the face. He was so furious with him that he had to leave the room.

Ray went upstairs to check on Cheryl. She had fallen asleep in her clothes. Her shoes were still on her feet. Removing them, he pulled the covers over her and laid next to her.

* * *

Whitney's mom helped Kia out the car and to the front door of her apartment. "Do you want us to stay while you tell your mother?" she asked. Kia shook her head no. "Alright, but if you need us, call."

Before opening the door to their apartment, Kia took a deep breath. It was about to be on and poppin' and she knew it. Walking quietly past the dining room, she headed straight to her room.

"Hey, wait a minute," her mother said, from the kitchen. Gwen turned off the stove. "How was the party?"

"It was okay," Kia said, still walking toward her bedroom.

Curious about her daughter's behavior, Gwen followed her to her room. She saw from the look on Kia's face, that something was seriously wrong. Gwen asked Kia to sit down.

"I want you to talk to me. Did something happen at the party?" Gwen asked.

"No," Kia said, holding the lab results behind her back.

"Well then, what's wrong with you? You look like you just lost your best friend. I thought you were past all this depression stuff."

Kia couldn't find the words to tell her mother she was pregnant. Instead, she handed her the lab results from the hospital.

"What's this?" Gwen asked, looking at the paper. Her jaw dropped after she scanned the paper and read the word *positive* beside the HCG blood test. Before Kia knew it, her mother was yelling at the top of her lungs.

"How could you be so dumb? Do you have any idea what you've done?"

Kia didn't say anything, she just sat quietly as tears welled up in her eyes, and her lips started to shiver.

"Oh God! How could you allow yourself to get caught up like the rest of the girls in this neighborhood? I thought you were smarter than that, Kia. YOU'RE ONLY FOURTEEN!" she yelled so loud, that Kia couldn't help but jump. Pacing back and forth, Gwen felt like she was in the twilight zone. *This can't be happening,* she thought. "And what's James gonna say?" Gwen yelled.

What's James gonna say? Kia thought. *What can he say? I ain't his child.* "Ma, this is a family matter. This has nothin' to do with him."

"How can you say that? Like it or not, he's a part of this family. He pays the bills, so he has the right to know what's going on under this roof," Gwen said, before walking out of Kia's room fuming.

Kia laid across her bed and cried herself to sleep. She knew she had let her mother down big time, and there was nothing she could do about it. Her dreams of going to college were going to have to be put on hold, and all because of one stupid mistake. Things got worse when James got home and Gwen told him the news.

"I told you that girl was hot in the pants," he said.

"James, she made a mistake. It was her first time."

"I thought you had her on something."

"Well, I never thought she needed any type of birth control. She's only fourteen, and I thought she was smarter than that."

Oh God! Could it be? Nah! James thought to himself.

The next day, Gwen called the Bensons and arranged a meeting with them. Because of their busy schedules, they weren't able to meet with them until the end of the week.

For the next three days, Gwen didn't say a word to Kia. She wouldn't even look at her. Kia had caused a big rift between Gwen and James. He wanted Gwen to put her out, and when she refused, he threatened to leave. Of course, he was just blowing off smoke. He would be a fool to leave a woman who worshiped the ground he walked on, cooked and cleaned for him, and put up with all his crap. Besides, who else would take him in?

Kia couldn't sleep the night before the meeting with Andre's parents. All she could think about was what a mess everything was. Her mother was mad at her, and she wasn't allowed to talk to Andre. Every time he would call, James would hang up on him.

Around nine the next morning, Kia's burning eyes opened

to James sitting on her bed.

"What are you doin' in my room?" she asked startled. She jumped up and covered herself. "Where's my mom?"

"She's in the shower," he said, pushing her down on the bed. "You just remember something. I'ma do all the talking when your little boyfriend's uppity parents get here. Don't you say a word!" he said, before leaving her room.

Kia sat on the edge of her bed. She daydreamed of she and Andre raising their baby together. She pictured them even living in his parent's home, and them treating her like part of the family. Unfortunately, she knew that would never happen. Not in a million years.

When Andre and his parents pulled up in front of Kia's building, his father shook his head. "Please tell me you don't hang out over here?" he asked, turning to Andre.

"You know what Dad, everyone is not…forget it!" Andre said, on the verge of losing it.

Exiting the car, a kid on a bike almost ran Ray down. "Hey, watch it!" he yelled.

"Shut up, ole man!" the kid yelled, as he kept on riding.

Concerned for their safety, he and his wife rushed into Kia's building. Andre walked behind them slowly. *What a joke, he's even scared of a little kid on a bike.*

Knock, knock, knock.

"Who is it? Kia said softly.

"It's me, Andre."

Kia's heart skipped a beat as she opened the door. This was the first time she had seen Andre since she found out she was carrying his child. He looked so good in his Lacoste shirt and his faded Old Navy jeans. His mother and father followed him into the apartment.

"How are you feeling?" Mrs. Benson asked, after giving Kia a hug.

"Yeah, how you feelin'?" Andre added, looking down at Kia's stomach.

"I'm a'ight," she said, glad Andre was concerned about her.

Gwen and James walked into the living room, introduced themselves, and sat down on the sofa. Mr. Benson, not being one to hold his tongue, started the conversation.

"I know this is a difficult situation for all of us, but we need to pull together to help Kia and Andre get through this ordeal."

Mrs. Benson was surprised by her husband's remarks, because he'd been dead set against Andre having anything to do with Kia and the baby. Now he was saying he was going to help in anyway he could.

"Well, I think we need to find out what they both plan on doing first. Kia hasn't even decided if she is gonna keep the baby," Gwen said.

Andre interjected. "With all due respect, Mrs. Tibbs, this is my baby too. I think we should be makin' that decision together," he said.

"Y'all don't need no baby! Ain't neither one of you ready for that," James huffed loudly, surprising everyone.

Andre went over and sat close to Kia. He took her hand and said, "Kia, this is your decision. Whatever you decide, I'll support you one hundred percent."

Kia was touched. She stared at him, her eyes wide. "What about school?" she asked.

"Yeah, and daycare, diapers and medical bills. Do you kids have any idea what it cost to take care of a baby these days?" Mr. Benson said.

"I'll just have to get a job," Andre said.

"And what, drop out of school? I don't think so. This is your last year, and then it's off to college for you," his father said.

"So, what are you saying? That Kia should take care of this baby by herself?" Gwen said, with an attitude.

"Mrs. Tibbs, my husband isn't saying that at all."

"Okay, then what is he saying?" James said, looking like a mad dog.

"I'm saying that our son has a bright future ahead of him, and he's not gonna throw it all away," Mr. Benson said, in his defense.

"Oh, and my daughter doesn't?" Gwen asked.

"Okay, will everyone just settle down for a minute. I think we're getting a little out of hand," Mrs. Benson pleaded.

Andre, fed up, looked at his parents, Gwen and James. "Look, we made a mistake, and now we have to deal with it. I'm gonna get a job and take care of my baby, with or without your help."

This was the proudest his mother had ever been of Andre. He made his mistake, and was ready to take responsibility for his actions. In her eyes, not too many young men would've done that.

Kia glanced at her mother. "I know I let you down, but I can still go to high school and college."

"Yeah, I'm disappointed in you, but the fact that you're willing to take accountability for what has happened, has made me rethink this whole thing." She kissed Kia on the cheek. Tears fell from Gwen's eyes. "Hey, we've all made mistakes, but we learn from them, and I hope you and Andre have learned from yours."

"Well, I guess we're about to be grandparents." Mr. Benson laughed.

"I guess so." Kia's mother smiled.

Everyone seemed to be in good spirits, except James. He gave Gwen a stabbing stare then walked out, slamming the door behind him. Mr. Benson was mystified by his behavior. *What is his problem? Kia is still going to school, and we're all going to pitch in and help. It isn't like he has to take care of the child by himself.*

"I have a private practice in Mitchellville, Maryland. I can take care of her prenatal care. After the baby is born, we'll have the baby added to our insurance plan," Mrs. Benson said. She looked at Kia's mother. "That's if it's alright with you."

"I don't see that I have a choice at this point, I can't afford it," Gwen said, feeling ashamed of her financial status.

"Kia, I'll set up an appointment for you next week in my office. My receptionist will call you with the time and day," Mrs. Benson said, as they stood up to leave.

"Thank you," Kia said, almost in tears. The whole ordeal was too much for her to bear.

* * *

The day of her appointment with Mrs. Benson, Kia had to go by herself. It was the day her mother's boss was deciding who to give the promotion to, so calling out wasn't an option for Gwen, especially with another mouth to feed.

With all the buses running later than usual due to an accident, Kia was late. By the time she got there, she was exhausted. She entered the office to find Andre and his mother talking in the receptionist area.

"You made it," Andre said, when she walked in.

"I'm sorry I'm late. I almost turned around and went back home when the bus took forever."

"I told you I would've picked you up," Andre said.

"I know, but I didn't want to bother you."

"You're not bothering me. This is my baby too, you know."

The middle aged, gray-haired nurse took Kia and Andre into one of the examining rooms. She took Kia's vitals then instructed her to get undressed. Moments later, Mrs. Benson entered and explained to them the examination she was about to perform.

"I'm going to give you an ultrasound. That's a harmless procedure, which shows the fetus, and makes it possible to obtain information about the fetus, like the size and any abnormalities. Then we'll go from there."

Kia laid back on the table. Holding Andre's hand, she watched as Mrs. Benson started the examination. Her silence made Kia and Andre nervous.

"Ma, what do you see?" Andre asked.

"Well, right here is your baby's head, and right here are the feet," she said, pointing to the monitor.

Andre and Kia smiled. This was truly an unreal experience for them. They were seeing their baby for the first time.

"Does it say when it's comin'?" Kia asked.

"You mean your due date?" Mrs. Benson asked, correcting Kia. "Yes, it does. By my calculations, your bundle of joy should be here sometime in April."

"What does that mean?" Andre asked curiously.

"That means Kia is four weeks." Kia and Andre stared at one another.

"That's impossible, she should be at least two months. We had sex in June."

Mrs. Benson was stunned at Andre's revelation. She even took another look, to make sure she wasn't misreading the ultrasound. "No, by my calculations, Kia is only four weeks."

Kia started to sob hysterically. Suddenly she knew that if she was only four weeks, the baby couldn't be Andre's. Which led her to the conclusion that it could only be one other person. The thought of being pregnant with his child made her throw up her breakfast.

"Kia, this baby isn't mine, is it?" Andre said, throwing the examination tray against the wall. He grabbed her by the arms and shook her. "So, whose baby is it?"

"Andre, calm down," his mother said, pulling her son away from Kia. "Let her get dressed, then we can go into my office and talk about this."

"No, we're gonna talk about this now!" Andre yelled, frantically pacing the floor. "Whose baby is it?" he screamed at the top of his lungs, scaring Kia. Andre wouldn't let up. "You acted like you were so scared of having sex, but I guess that was all an act. Huh…Huh! Say something!"

Mrs. Benson started to get concerned when she saw Kia's eyes closing. "Kia, are you alright?"

"He told me not to tell anyone. He said it was our little secret," she said, in a trance like state.

"Who? Kia, you have to talk to me. That's the only way I can help you," Mrs. Benson said, holding her hand. Kia opened her eyes and looked straight at Andre.

"I was asleep on my bed when he came into my room. I told him to leave, but he wouldn't."

"Who are you talking about? What did he do?" Mrs. Benson asked, afraid to hear the answer.

"He put his hands over my mouth and pull my shorts down. Then he…he…" She began to sob hysterically. It took several minutes for Andre and his mother to calm her down.

Mrs. Benson knew what Kia was trying to tell her and it made her sick. Kia had been violated in the worst way. She had been raped.

"Kia, who did this to you?" Andre asked, ready to tear someone's head off.

"He told me not to tell or he'd hurt my mom."

Mrs. Benson began to get angry. "Kia, I promise you, we won't let anything happen to your mother, but you have to trust me. Tell me who did this. He needs to pay for what he did to you."

Kia didn't speak, instead her mind drifted back to that

dreadful night.

After talking to Kia for more than an hour about incest and child abuse, and how important it is for the victim not to feel responsible for what has happened to them, Kia finally felt strong enough to tell Mrs. Benson who the perpetrator was.

"It was James, my stepfather. He raped me!"

Mrs. Benson felt sick to her stomach. *How could a grown man take advantage of a young girl like that?* "Kia, I know this is hard for you, but you need to tell your mother, so she can call the police."

"No! I don't want anyone to know!" Kia said, sitting up. "He might hurt my mother if I tell the police."

"I promise you, if you tell the police what happened, he won't be able to hurt you or your mother ever again."

Kia sat quietly for a minute then asked if she could go home.

"Sweetheart, I can't let you go home. I'm obligated by law to inform Child Protective Services and the police what you just told me. Your stepfather needs to pay for what he's done to you." Mrs. Benson walked to the door, then turned around and looked at Kia. "I'm sorry, I have no choice but to report this."

Kia stood up, slid her jeans on under her hospital gown and walked towards the door.

"Where you goin'?" Andre asked, confused.

"I'm gonna call Whitney, so she can come and give me a ride home," Kia said, on the brink of crying again.

Feeling bad about the way he treated her, Andre walked over and embraced Kia. "You're the strongest person I know. You can do this." He hugged her tighter. "You need to do this so it doesn't happen to someone else."

Although she was scared, she knew Andre and his mother were right. So she agreed to report the incident to the police.

Mrs. Benson went into her office and called Kia's mother at

work.

"Hello, Gwen, it's Cheryl Benson," she said, after Gwen picked up the phone.

"Hi, Cheryl, is everything alright with Kia?" Gwen asked.

"Gwen, I'm afraid not."

"Oh, my God, what's wrong?" she said panicking.

"Kia has to tell you something. We need you to meet us at the First District police station."

"The police station? What's going on? You're scaring me."

"We'll explain everything when we get there."

"I'm leaving right now," Gwen said, with fear in her voice.

Andre, Mrs. Benson, and Kia piled into Mrs. Benson's Mercedes and headed to the police station. When they got there, seeing Gwen's face made Kia freeze up again. She nearly had a breakdown when the officer came out and asked her and Gwen to follow her.

"Kia, it's going to be alright," Mrs. Benson said, holding her hand. "We're going to be right here when you come out."

Sitting in the interrogation room made Kia feel like she was the criminal, instead of the victim.

"Hi, my name is Detective Richards," the female officer said, extending her hand to Kia and Gwen. "Mrs. Tibbs, the reason we asked you down here is because your daughter was sexually assaulted in July."

"What? There must be some mistake. Kia never mentioned anything about being assaulted to me."

"Ma'am, most kids don't. They fear no one will believe them, and most of the time, they feel like they asked for it."

"Okay, this is just too much. First you get pregnant, now this," Gwen said confused.

Kia sensed her mother's anger, and walked towards the door. Detective Richards stopped her. "Kia, I know this is very difficult for you, but I need you to tell me and your mother everything that happened that night."

Detective Richards' calm, concerning demeanor and friendly face was something Kia wasn't used to seeing from cops in her neighborhood. She made her feel safe, so safe that she felt strong enough to talk about the night she was raped.

Sobbing throughout the interview, Kia ended it by saying, "I told him no, but he wouldn't stop."

"Who wouldn't stop?" Gwen asked. "Who?"

"James!"

Gwen was so shocked, she almost passed out. "What do you mean James?" She was livid. "Kia, James would never do something like that. Never!"

"Well, he did, Ma! He raped me!"

"Oh God!!!" Gwen said, grabbing her head.

The story angered Detective Richards. "Kia, I want you to know this isn't your fault. You said no and no means no." She knew that prosecuting a rape case would be hard. Not having any physical evidence would make it even harder. Nevertheless, she took what she had to the District Attorney in the Special Victims Unit and asked for an arrest warrant for James.

After securing the warrant, Detective Richards, two officers, Kia, Mrs. Tibbs, Mrs. Benson and Andre drove to Kia's apartment to confront James. Kia was scared to death. Gwen, on the other hand, was on a warpath.

Standing outside the door, Detective Richards told Gwen to let them handle it from here. "I know it's hard, but you have to let the legal system take care of him," she said to Gwen.

When Gwen walked in the door, James was seated on the couch watching television. After he saw the police standing there, he got up and walked over to Gwen.

"What's going on?" he asked. He looked at Kia. "What did you do now?"

Kia said nothing, but her body was visibly shaken.

Gwen couldn't contain herself any longer. She turned and punched James so hard she knocked out his two front teeth. Everyone was shocked.

"What's wrong with you? Why did you hit me?" James yelled, stunned.

"Because you raped me!" Kia stood in front of James. "What you did to me haunts me every night, and it's probably gonna haunt me for the rest of my life. Hopefully, you'll spend the rest of your life in jail thinking about it too."

"You pathetic animal!" Gwen screamed, as she broke down in tears. "How could you do that to my baby?"

"Baby, come on. She's lying. You know I wouldn't do something like that. She's just tryna break us up."

Kia intervened. "Ma, the baby I'm carrying isn't Andre's, it's James. I'm tellin' you the truth."

Gwen's jaw dropped. "What?" she said, turning to Kia.

"It's not Andre's, it's James' baby."

Gwen turned to James with tears in her eyes. "It's your baby?" she asked, in total shock.

"You little...stop lying," James said, reaching for Kia's neck.

The police quickly grabbed James and handcuffed him as Detective Richards read him his rights.

Gwen was so mad at herself for not seeing what Kia had been through. The mood swings, the anger, nightmares, depression, and avoiding her friends, were all signs that she had been raped. Unfortunately, Gwen didn't know that. She looked Kia in the eyes and asked for her forgiveness.

"Forgive you for what?" Kia asked confused. "Mama, you didn't do anything."

"That's just it. I didn't protect you. I'll never let something like this happen again. I promise you."

The two hugged as the police led James out the apartment

and into a squad car. Andre and Mrs. Benson stayed behind to comfort the two.

* * *

Six months later, James pleaded guilty to raping Kia. During her testimony at the sentencing hearing, in front of a packed courtroom, Kia broke down as she told the judge how James raped her, and how he threatened to hurt her and her mother if she told anyone.

"I said no, but he wouldn't stop," she cried, looking directly at James sitting at the table with his attorney. After her testimony, there wasn't a dry eye in the courtroom.

Next, Gwen came into the courtroom, and spoke about the physical abuse she had endured from James. She begged the judge to sentence James to the maximum sentence allowable, so that he couldn't do this any other teenager.

The judge, after hearing Kia and Gwen make appealing statements to throw the book at James, sentenced him to ten years in prison and five years supervised probation. When Kia heard that, she smiled for the first time in over six months. Andre was right beside her, holding her hand. She knew that with counseling, God's help, and Andre's love, she would recover from this ordeal.

Kia had lost the baby in the third month of her pregnancy, due to all the stress she was going through. In the end, she felt it was for the best because she knew if she hadn't, there was no way that she could look at her baby everyday without reliving the rape.

She returned to school and even started a group called TASAR — Taking A Stand Against Rapists. She wanted to help teens, who had been through the same or a similar situation, get through it like she did.

Teenage Bluez II

All Alone
by Darnell C. Jackson

On a warm Thursday afternoon, Mahogany had just gotten home from school. She sat in the living room of their spacious home in the Overbrook section of Philadelphia, which was furnished with an off-white leather, three-sectional sofa and matching love seat. The coffee and end tables were made of off-white oak wood. There was a 32-inch plasma television in one corner, and in the other, was a state of the art entertainment system. The dining room furniture was made of light brown oak, and in the kitchen they had all state of the art appliances in black lacquer.

Mahogany loved her home, and felt blessed to be living with both of her parents. She was their only child, and got basically any and everything she desired. Her father loved his little girl, and spoiled her every chance he got. Some of her friends were either living with their mother or grandparents, and most times, their father was either not in the picture or locked up.

She was waiting at the window for her father, Donte, to arrive. When she saw his 2003 Mercedes ML350 SUV coming down the street, she got excited. She always looked forward to his arrival. But as he was parking, she suddenly saw four police vehicles come racing down the street. Her eyes got wide as she saw the police surround her father's car. She ran to the door.

The police walked up to his car, with guns drawn. *Ah, man,* he said to himself. "What's up, officers?" Donte asked, trying to remain calm. He knew he had just picked up a package of dope, which was tucked under the back seat.

"Sir, please step out the car slowly," one of them said.

"What for? This is where I live," he said, pointing toward his house, and seeing Mahogany standing at the door. He could see the fear in her eyes.

"Sir, we just observed you leaving a well-known drug area in North Philly. Now will you step out the car?"

"So, if you saw me leaving a drug area in North Philly, why didn't you stop me then? Why follow me home?" Donte asked stalling.

"Because we've been watching you for sometime. We already know that you're dealing drugs. Now, I'm not gonna ask you again, step out the car!"

Donte got out his car, and looked at Mahogany, who was near tears by now. The police began to search his SUV, and it only took about a minute before they found the package.

"Sir, you're under arrest," the policeman said, placing handcuffs on Donte.

At this point, Mahogany ran down the steps screaming, "No, no! You can't arrest my Daddy!"

Another officer caught Mahogany as she was running toward Donte. "Sweetheart, I really hate for you to see this, but when people break the law, they will be arrested."

"But…but…my father wouldn't break the law," Mahogany cried.

"Mahogany, go inside and call you mother," Donte said, as he was being placed in the back of the police car.

"Daddy!!!" Mahogany screamed, as he was being driven away. She stood on the sidewalk, crying uncontrollably.

A policeman walked up to her and said, "Sweetheart, go inside and call your mother. Tell her that we've taken your father down to the 19th Police District. Again, I'm really sorry you had to see this."

By this time, some of her neighbors were standing on their porches, but she didn't care about them. Mahogany, still crying, walked slowly in the house. She picked up the phone and dialed her mother's job number.

"Hello, Tanya Johnson speaking. How can…"

Before she could finish her sentence, Mahogany screamed, "Mommy, they took Daddy away!!!"

"Mahogany? Slow down, baby. What are you talking about? Who took Daddy away?"

"The police, they arrested Daddy right in front of the house!"

"What?" She couldn't believe what she was hearing. "When? Where did they take him?"

"Just a few minutes ago, and they took him to the 19th Police District. Mommy, I'm scared. What's gonna happen to Daddy?" Mahogany said, still crying.

"Sweetheart, stop crying. Everything is gonna be alright," she said, even though she didn't know whether what she was saying to Mahogany was true or not. "I'm going down there right now. I'll call you as soon as I know something. Stay in the house," Tanya said, before hanging up the phone.

When she arrived at the 19th District, she was advised that Donte was being held on possession of drugs. *Drugs? That can't be right, my husband wouldn't be dealing drugs*, she said to herself.

"Ma'am, I think it would be best if you just went home, because your husband probably won't be seeing the judge for a couple of hours," the officer she spoke to said.

"Say what? He didn't do anything, so why can't he be released now?" she asked, still not understanding what was actually happening.

"Ma'am, I told you he's being held on drug possession, which is a serious charge. He might get bail, but I seriously doubt it. I'm sorry to have to tell you this, but we've been watching your husband for a while now, trying to get enough evidence on him. We have him on tape selling and buying drugs."

This can't be happening, Tanya thought. *How could Donte be a drug-dealer and I not know?*

She called Mahogany, and told her that everything was alright, and that she would be home in a little while. Even though she knew she was lying, she didn't want to upset Mahogany anymore than she already was.

By the time Tanya got home, Mahogany was asleep. A couple hours later, Donte called home.

"Hello," Tanya said, answering the phone on the first ring.

"Hey, baby," Donte said, in a strange voice. "What ya doin'?"

"What do you mean, what am I doing? What are you doing dealing drugs?" she yelled.

"Baby, calm down. It's not that serious. I'm gonna beat this bull crap charge. They can't prove the drugs were mine. Plus it was an illegal search," he said, trying to calm her down.

"Donte, that's bull! If they found drugs in your truck, they got you. Plus, the officer said they've been watching you for a while. Have they given you bail yet?"

"No, but hopefully I'll get to see the judge soon. Listen, I gotta go. Remember, I love you, baby."

After Tanya hung up, she sat at the kitchen table and started crying. She couldn't believe that Donte had gotten caught up in the drug game. She couldn't figure out how he had been able to hide this from her. She wondered how long he'd been dealing drugs. *How could I have been so stupid?* Now she had to worry about him having to do time, while she was left to take care of

Mahogany and their home. *What am I gonna do?* she thought to herself.

Donte didn't come home until the wee hours of the morning. When he walked in, Tanya was sitting in the living room wide-awake.

"Baby, I'm glad to see they let you out on bail," she said, jumping up and hugging him. "So, what happens now?"

"I have a preliminary hearing comin' up, and then they'll decide whether I'm gonna have to stand trial."

"Why don't you just plead guilty? Maybe the judge will go easy on you." She didn't know what else to say, because she was scared to death.

"Baby, I can't do that."

"Why not?"

"Because if I do, the judge will throw the book at me. Plus, I told you the drugs weren't mine."

"Donte, stop lying! How long have you been dealing drugs?"

He looked at her and knew he had to come clean, because he was facing some serious time, and he didn't want to lose her or his daughter.

"Do you remember when I got laid off a year ago? Well, a buddy of mine told me that if I hooked him up with some coke, he'd take care of me. Since my unemployment wasn't that much, I figured I'd do it that one time, but the money was easy and it got good to me. Next thing I knew, I was out there buying and selling for myself."

"What? How did you know where to get that stuff from? Also, how could you hide it from me for over a year? I don't understand," Tanya cried. "You told me you'd gotten a job. You left home every evening. I can't believe I was that stupid."

"My homeboy is into selling to dealers, and I hooked him up with my buddy. Baby, I had to tell you those lies, because I wasn't gonna bring no drugs into our home. I thought I could get out just as fast as I got in the game, but I was wrong. Sweetie, I'm so sorry for bringing you this drama."

"Donte, if you're convicted, what am I gonna do?"

"Listen, let's not talk about that."

* * *

It was 3:30 in the afternoon when Mahogany came in from school and found her mother, Tanya, slumped over on the sofa. She looked down at her and thought, *Please, Lord, don't let her be dead this time.* Mahogany cautiously walked over to her mother, afraid to even touch her for fear that her body would be cold. She stood over her for a minute, trying to figure out if she was breathing.

Mahogany had grown into a beautiful sixteen-year old teenager; 5'7, with long slender legs and jet-black hair, that came down to her shoulders. Her skin was absolutely flawless and she had an hourglass figure. Her friends were always telling her that she could be a model. Sometimes she'd stand in front of the mirror in her bedroom and pretend she was on *America's Next Top Model.*

She hadn't seen her father since she was thirteen. That is when he was found guilty of drug possession, with intent to distribute, and sentenced to ten years without any chance of parole. Since he had been locked up, she felt like she was living someone else's life. All the good times were gone, and there was no one there for her, not even her mother. She remembered one summer when she was twelve, and her father took them down to Wildwood, New Jersey for the weekend.

Donte came in the house on a Friday, and said, "Honey, you and Mahogany pack your bags, we're going to Wildwood for the weekend."

"For real, Daddy!" Mahogany yelled, who was sitting in the living room with her mother.

"Yeah. Get your stuff so we can get on the road." He smiled.

Tanya walked over to Donte and kissed him on the lips. *"Sweetie, this is a nice surprise. And we just heard the weather this weekend is gonna be great."*

"Okay, so let's get a move on. I want to get a tan." Tanya laughed at that statement, because Donte was already dark chocolate. He stood 6 feet, with a baldhead, and a serious six-pack for a thirty-seven year old.

"Sweetie, the last thing you need is to be in a sun," Tanya said, going upstairs to pack their bags.

Tanya, who was thirty-five at the time, stood 5 feet 7, with long slender legs like Mahogany, and her complexion was milk chocolate. She had put on a little weight in the past year, but not much. She wore her hair in micro-braids.

After everyone's bags were packed, they got into Donte's SUV. On the drive down, Mahogany and Donte played the *"Name That Car"* game, in which Mahogany won hands down.

"You know this game too good. Don't let me find out you ridin' around in cars with some knucklehead boy," Donte laughed.

"Come on, Daddy, you know you're the only man in my life," Mahogany said smiling.

A couple rest stops later, they pulled into the Port Royal Hotel on the Beach in Wildwood, New Jersey. After checking in, they changed and went down to the beach. While Tanya laid on the beach, Donte and Mahogany frolicked in the ocean.

That weekend was one of Mahogany's fondest memories, and whenever she was really missing her dad, she would go back there because it would give her comfort.

Back then she could also talk to her mom about anything. When she was little, her father would tuck her in bed at night and read her a bedtime story. They were like a real family. But a year after he went to jail, the light in her mom's eyes seemed to die out.

Around that time, Mahogany started noticing that her mom was drinking more than normal. Prior to that time, she would occasionally have a glass of wine with dinner. But now, she was either out clubbing and drinking, or at home drinking alone. She no longer cared what Mahogany did, where she went, or whom she hung out with. It seemed all she cared about was where her next drink was coming from.

When Donte first went to jail, Tanya would visit him every visiting day. She would try and convince Mahogany to go with her, but she wasn't interested in seeing her father behind bars, so she would always find an excuse not to go. Tanya would write to him three times a week, and anytime he called collect, she would accept his calls, no matter what time is was.

After doing this for a year, the emotional and physical strain started to take a toll on her. At first, she started going out after work with friends. Then Mahogany started seeing a change in her mother. She would come in from work, and the first thing she reached for was a Colt 45 and a glass of Seagram's vodka straight. Before Mahogany knew it, her mother's drinking had gotten out of control. She was no longer visiting Donte as often as she had a year ago. Whenever he called, they always ended up arguing, because he knew something wasn't right with Tanya.

Tanya loved her daughter, but doing this all alone was becoming too much for her to handle, especially now that Mahogany was sixteen. She hadn't been with another man in three years because she still loved her husband, even though she knew he was gonna be in jail for another seven years. She was so lonely, and felt the only way to ease her pain was to drown it in alcohol. Tanya knew that Mahogany was hurting and missing her father, but because of her own pain, she didn't take notice of the change in her daughter until it was almost too late.

Mahogany finally got up the nerve to touch her mother. "Mom, Mom, are you alright?"

"Yeah. What do you want?" Tanya slurred, waking up.

"Nothin'. I just wanted to let you know I'm home. And in case you care, my day was good. I got an A on my math test." Looking down at her drunken mother, she wished for the good old days.

"That's good, baby," Tanya said, sitting up on the sofa. She looked around, trying to figure out what time of day it was.

"Mom, why are you home so early?" Mahogany asked.

"I took a half day. Is that alright with you? And being as though I'm grown, I can take off when I feel like it. Now take your butt in the kitchen and get me a beer," Tanya said, reaching for the bottle of Seagram's on the coffee table.

"Okay, but if you keep takin' days off from work, aren't you afraid you might get fired?" Mahogany asked, really concerned. Lately, her mother was either not going to work due to her having a hangover, or leaving work early.

"I've been working for that bank too long. Plus, I have the time, so why can't I use it," Tanya said. She was a Loan Officer at Citibank in Center City Philadelphia. She had been there for over ten years, so she wasn't worried about being fired.

Mahogany shook her head and said, "Whatever, but when you get fired and we lose everything, don't say nothin' to me." She turned and walked into the kitchen.

"Keep getting smart and I'ma slap the taste outta your mouth!" Tanya said, starting to stand up.

"Chill out, Mom. I'm sorry. I'm goin' upstairs to do my homework," she said, coming back into the living room, and slamming the beer down on the coffee table.

"Slam one more thing in my house, and I'ma slam your

butt!" Tanya said, reaching for the television remote control. Tanya knew how she was treating and ignoring her daughter wasn't right, but she just couldn't handle all of this alone anymore.

Shaking her head, Mahogany went upstairs, mumbling under her breath. *If you stop drinkin', then I wouldn't be slammin' things down on the table.*

"And when you're done your homework, get your butt back down here and start dinner!" Tanya yelled up to Mahogany.

Mahogany slammed her bedroom door and said to herself, *I hope she don't hold her breath waitin' on me to cook dinner, cause her butt will die of hunger.*

Mahogany was in the eleventh grade and attended Dobbins High School, located at 22nd and Lehigh Avenue in North Philadelphia. The stuff that was going on at home was affecting her so bad, that her grade point average dropped from a 3.9 to a 3.0. She couldn't concentrate at school, because she was always so worried about whether her mother would come straight home from work, or when she finally did come home, what condition she would be in.

She remembered many nights when her mother came home so drunk, that she had to help her upstairs, get her undressed and into bed. All of this was becoming too much for her, and in return, she turned her anger toward her father. Because if he hadn't been out there selling drugs and gotten arrested, then maybe her mother wouldn't be a drunk.

She knew it was wrong of her not to answer any of her dad's letters, but she just couldn't bring herself to tell him how much she missed him, and how angry she was at him for leaving them. She was angry because he chose to sell drugs over loving her. Now she felt all alone, because not only didn't she have him around, but she was losing her mother to alcohol. She was tired of crying herself to sleep because she missed her father so much.

After she finished trying to do her homework, which wasn't a complete success, she cut on her computer and checked her e-mails. Then she called her best friend, Bianca, to see what she was up to.

"Hello," Bianca said, answering her phone.

"Hey, girl. What ya doin'?"

"Nothin', sitting her bored to death. What ya doin'?"

"Tryna get the heck up outta here because my mom's drunk again and trippin'. If I don't get out of here soon, I just might catch a case," Mahogany said laughing.

"Yeah, right. Why don't you come over and we'll go to the Gallery to check out the fellas. You got any money?" Bianca said.

"I got a lil' sumthin'. That sounds like a plan. Give me a minute. My mom wants me to cook dinner. But I figure if I wait long enough, she'll fall back into the drunken stupor I found her in when I got home."

"We can't wait too long, cause you know the Gallery closes at seven, and it's already 4:45. To avoid an argument, and then your mom not lettin' you go, why don't you just fix her somethin' to eat and leave it on the counter?" Bianca said.

Bianca and Mahogany had known each other since they were nine, and they were best of friends. Bianca was 5'6, with a milk chocolate complexion, and a tiny waist. She kept her hair in micro-braids. She lived a couple blocks from Mahogany with both of her parents and little sister, who was six.

Bianca knew all about Mahogany's family history and was very supportive of her friend. She felt really bad for her and wished there was something she could do to make her life better. She even went to her mother about Mahogany's mom's excessive drinking, and how it was affecting Mahogany. Her mom told her to just be there for Mahogany, and that she would try and talk to Tanya.

"Yeah, you're right. Give me a half hour to throw somethin' together for her, and then I'll be at your house. We can jump on the train and be at the Gallery in ten minutes." Mahogany hung up and went downstairs.

"Mom, I'm goin' to the Gallery with Bianca. But before I go, I'ma fix you somethin' to eat and leave it on the counter for you, okay," she said.

"Yeah, whatever. But you better be home before your curfew," Tanya slurred, staring at the television, watching a rerun of *The Jeffersons* on cable. She sat on the sofa, wearing a pair of Donte's old sweatpants, and one of his t-shirts. Her hair was looking like she should have gotten a perm a week ago. It was all over the place, making her look like a deranged homeless person.

Mahogany stood in front of her mother, with her hands on her hips. "Mom, why do you drink so much? If you don't stop, you're gonna end up dead. Is that what you want to happen? Then who will I have?" she said, nearly in tears. She told herself that she would never take a drink or do drugs. She didn't want to end up her like her parents, no matter what curve life threw her.

"Baby, I got this under control, don't you worry. It's just that when I drink, I don't have to think about how lonely I am," Tanya said, starting to cry. She really didn't want her daughter to know how she really felt, and how she used alcohol as a band-aid.

"Mom, I miss Dad too, but you drinking isn't gonna bring him home any faster."

Part of her tried to understand how her mother felt, but what she couldn't understand was, didn't her mother care how she was feeling? Didn't she realize that she was missing her father also, and now with her drinking like she was, she had no one to turn to? Both sets of her grandparents were dead and gone, and all her aunts and uncles were in different states. If things didn't change soon, she knew she was gonna have no choice but to call her mother's older sister, Sheila, and ask for her help.

Sheila lived in Florida with her husband and two children. Even though Tanya loved Sheila with all her heart, she always felt Sheila thought she was better than her. Sheila's husband was a surgeon at a major hospital in Florida, and her children went to private school. Sheila didn't have to work. All she did was hang out with her rich friends all day, shopping, and getting tanned. No matter what Tanya did, Sheila was always judging her.

When she told her about Donte being arrested and sentenced to ten years in jail, Sheila immediately said, "I told you that man was no good from the get go."

Mahogany knew her mother wouldn't want Sheila to know how she was spiraling out of control, but she was at the point where she didn't know where to turn anymore.

"Why don't you call up one of your girlfriends and go see a movie or somethin'? All you do is go to work and drink. What kind of life is that? I know you miss Daddy, but he's not comin' home anytime soon. Are you gonna continue drinking like this until he comes home? By then you're gonna have cirrhosis of the liver or be dead. And then where will that leave me?" Mahogany cried.

"Chile, please. I don't drink everyday."

"Mom, yes you do. We never do anything together anymore. How about next weekend you and me do somethin'? Maybe we can go get our nails and feet done, and then have lunch in Chinatown. How does that sound?" Mahogany said. She really wanted to reconnect with her mother. She missed the person she used to be so much.

"Okay, if it'll get you off my back, we'll do that. Now get on outta here," Tanya said. She didn't need her child making her feel anymore guilty than she was already feeling.

After Mahogany left, Tanya downed the rest of her beer and went into the kitchen to see what she had left her to eat. On the stove was a plate of leftover fried chicken, fried rice and corn. She took the chicken breast off the plate and got another beer out the fridge and went back into the living room. She looked at the fifth of vodka, which was almost gone, and popped the tab on her beer. She quickly downed two shots of vodka, sat back on the sofa and channel surfed, not really watching anything in particular.

Tanya finished her beer, stumbled upstairs, and went into the bathroom to soak in the tub. By the time Mahogany came back home, Tanya had fallen asleep in the tub.

"Mom, wake up!" Mahogany yelled, as she shook her mother.

"Oh, you're home. I must've fallen asleep while taking a bath." Tanya started shaking because the water had turned cold.

"Yeah, right. Why would you take a bath and you're drunk? You could've drowned, Mom!" Mahogany cried.

"Chile, stop being so dramatic," Tanya said, grabbing the white fluffy towel lying on the toilet. She climbed out the tub.

"So, are you sayin' after I left, you didn't drink anything else?"

"I'm not saying that, but I wasn't drunk."

"Yeah, right. Mom, I know that Daddy being away is hard on you, but it's hard on me too. Do you think maybe you should go talk to someone? I'll go with you."

"Oh, so now you're saying I'm crazy."

"No, I'm just worried about you, that's all. I see you can't handle Daddy being in jail. And maybe talking to someone will help you with your problem."

"Mahogany, go to bed. You have school and I have to go to

work tomorrow. I don't have a problem. I just fell asleep in the tub," Tanya said, as she walked into her bedroom.

"Are you sure you're goin' to work tomorrow?"

"Why must you always be so difficult?"

"Mom, never mind. I don't care if you drink yourself into a comma," Mahogany said, leaving out the bathroom. She didn't really mean that, but that's how she was feeling at the moment.

*   *   *

When Mahogany got to her school locker the next day, Bianca was waiting for her. She immediately noticed something was wrong.

"Girl, why the long face?" she asked Mahogany.

"Do you know when I got home last night, my mom was drunk and asleep in the tub."

"Say what?" Bianca said.

"You heard me. That stuff scared me to death. When I walked into the bathroom, I thought she was dead. I don't know how much more of this I can handle," Mahogany cried. "I even suggested she go see someone, but she told me she had everythin' under control. With all the stress she's causin' me, I'm startin' to feel like I need a drink," Mahogany said, with a straight face.

"Mahogany, don't even play like that. You see what that stuff does to you, just look at your mother," Bianca said, not liking the look on her friend's face. "Do you want my mom to try and talk to your mom again?"

"Naw, it's not gonna do any good. I'm at the point where I don't care anymore. Look, I have to get to class before I'm late. I'll talk to you at lunch." Mahogany closed her locker, and went to her next class, which was Math.

She sat in class, not hearing a thing her teacher was saying.

Keith, who was fine, nudged Mahogany to get her attention. He'd had a thing for her since last year, but she never seemed to give him the time of day. But lately, he could see that she had something on her mind, so he figured this was a good time to try and get next to her.

He decided to see how far he could get with her. He said, "Hey girl, you seem a little down today. Wanna talk about it?"

Mahogany looked at him, and since she was feeling lonely and starving for attention, she played right into his hand. "Yeah, I'm a little down, but nothin' I care to talk about," Mahogany said, smiling at him.

"See, you have a pretty smile, you should do it more often," he said, turning on the charm.

Keith was 6'2, and a dark chocolate brotha. He was the star on the basketball team. He knew he was the reason their record was 6 and 0. Learning came easy to him, but he was definitely a playa with the ladies. All the girls were after him, but he only had his sight set on getting Mahogany. He wasn't into selling drugs or anything like that, and he had no intention of getting into the game. He was on his way to college on a basketball scholarship after he graduated.

She told herself, *Darn, he's fine, and it would be great to have someone to talk to.*

"So, what you doin' after school?" Keith asked her.

"Nothin' really, why?"

"Wanna hang out at my house for a while?" When Keith saw her hesitation, he said, "No pressure. We can just sit, talk and watch some music videos." He was playing his role to a tee.

"Maybe, I'm not sure. After school catch up with me at my locker, it's on the second floor," she said.

When school ended, Mahogany caught up with Bianca and told her what Keith had said to her. Bianca said, "Girl, you know Keith's reputation. Why are you even feeding into his bull?" Lately she had seen a change in Mahogany that she didn't like.

For the past couple months, she no longer seemed to care about school, and her grades were starting to drop. It frustrated Bianca that her friend was hurting and there wasn't anything she could do because Mahogany was starting to shut her out.

"Bianca, my dad's locked up, and my mom is in her own world. So if Keith wants to be there for me, what's the harm?"

"The harm is he has a reputation around school. He doesn't care about you, he only wants to get the draws."

"And what's wrong with that? At least someone will care how I feel."

"Mahogany, don't do this. Come home with me, talk to my mom," Bianca said, afraid for her friend.

"I appreciate your concern, but this is my life, and I wanna have some fun. I'm tired of worryin' about my parents and their problems. Maybe tonight I'll get good and drunk. Who knows, it might help me understand why my mom likes drinking so much."

"Mahogany, that's not the answer and you know it," Bianca said.

Just then Keith walked up to them and said, "Well, have you decided to hang out wit' me today or what?"

Mahogany looked at Keith, then at Bianca, whose eyes were pleading with her not to go with him.

"C'mon, Keith, let's bounce. Bianca, I'll call you later," she said, closing her locker.

"Okay, girl. Make sure you call me later tonight," Bianca said, as she watched them walk away. She had a really bad feeling, and she wanted to grab Mahogany and drag her away from Keith. But she knew it wouldn't do any good.

Mahogany and Keith walked out to his 2004 black Maxima. Keith said, "So, I see your girl isn't too happy 'bout you hangin' out wit' me." He looked at her with a smile that temporarily made her forget all about her troubles at home.

"No she's not. But since she's not my mother, I guess I can hang wit' ya for a minute," Mahogany said, trying to sound hip, but inside she was shaking.

When they got to his car, one of his boys rode up and said, "Man, guess there's no need for me to holla at you later." He had a knowing smile on his face, like he knew what Keith was up to.

"I'll holla at ya later," Keith said.

She knew going over Keith's house wasn't a smart thing, but since she was craving for some attention, she didn't listen to the little voice in her head. She also knew her mother would have a fit if she didn't make it home before her. Mahogany decided to call her mother at work.

"Let me make a call before we roll," she said to Keith.

"Handle ya business," he said, opening the car door and getting in.

Mahogany walked a little ways from the car and pulled out her cell phone. She dialed her mom's job number.

"Hello, can I speak to Ms. Tanya Johnson, this is her daughter, Mahogany," she said, once the receptionist answered the phone.

"One moment please," the receptionist said.

While she was waiting for her mother to pick up, Mahogany thought about what she would say to her. *I'll tell her that I'm goin' over Bianca's house to study for a test tomorrow. Or maybe I'll...* Before she could finish her thought, her mother got on the line.

"Hey, sweetie, what's up?"

"Hey, Mom. I just wanted to let you know I'm goin' over to Bianca's house. We have a big history test tomorrow and we're going to study together." She looked back at Keith while she was talking, and he nodded his head and smiled. *Oh man, I hope*

*my mom doesn't give me a hard time, cause that brotha is fine.
I don't care what his reputation around school is.*

"Okay. I'ma be a little late myself. Me and the girls are gonna stop for a quick drink after work," Tanya said. "Just make sure you don't come in too late."

"So what else is new?" Mahogany mumbled.

"What?" Tanya asked, not really hearing her.

"Nothin'. I said I won't be too late."

"Okay. I'll talk to you later. I have to get back to work, cause I have a client coming in about five minutes," Tanya said.

"Whatever. I'll see you later, Mom," she said, hanging up and returning to the car. "Let's roll," she said to Keith, who was sitting in his car listening to the radio.

"Everythin' cool?" he asked her.

"Yeah. Let's just get outta here." She sat staring out the window. Right now all she wanted to do was escape from her life. She knew by the time she got home, her mom would either not be there or passed out drunk.

She asked Keith, "Do you have any sisters or brothers?"

"Yeah, I have an older brother, but he's in jail. My parents think because I hang in the streets, I'm gonna end up like him. I keep tellin' them I'm not into that stuff, I just like havin' fun, but they're always on my back. Right now I have colleges knockin' my door down, wanting me to come play for them when I graduate."

"Do you speak to your brother?" Hearing him say that he had a family member in jail, made her heart beat fast. She couldn't believe she had found someone who she could relate to. It no longer bothered her that he had a reputation as a ladies man around school.

"We speak once in a while," he said.

"My dad's in jail," she said quietly.

"Word? What he do?"

"Three years ago he got busted for having drugs in his car. Come to find out, he was sellin' drugs all along. Ever since then, things at home haven't been right. I will never get involved with a man who sells drugs, because quick money can only lead to incarceration. I would rather struggle with my man, than have to visit him behind bars."

"Man, that's rough. But I feel you. Maybe I can take your mind off your troubles for a while," he said smiling.

They drove in silence until they pulled up to his house on 29th & Lehigh Avenue. It was a two-story, white row house. He parked the car, and they walked up the steps to his house.

Mahogany said, "Keith, I didn't know you lived so close to the school."

"Boo, there's a lot of things you don't know about me. Let's go inside so we can get to know each other better," he said, opening the front door and going inside.

Mahogany followed behind him, looking into each room they passed. From what she could see, Keith and his family were living pretty good. In the living room, which was on the right, there was a light brown leather sofa and recliner. The coffee and end tables were made of red cherry wood. On the walls were various pictures of Keith and his family.

The dining room table was set with a four-piece place setting. A china closet was on one wall, which contained some of the prettiest knick-knacks that Mahogany had ever seen.

She said, "Keith, I love your house. What do your parents do for a living?"

"My mom works for an accounting firm, and my dad owns a construction company. C'mon, we're goin' down to the basement. I fixed it up so I could have some privacy and chill wit' my boys."

When they got to the basement, Keith hit the light switch. Mahogany was impressed. In one corner, there was a black leather sofa and a 36-inch Sony plasma TV, with a DVD player, PS2, and on the rack right next to the television, there was every movie and PS2 game you could imagine. Over on the other side, there as a bomb stereo system, with a six-changer CD player attached to it.

At the other end of the basement, there was bar, which was fully stocked. Off to the right of the bar, was a bathroom.

"Man, this is nice," Mahogany said.

"Yeah, I call it my spot," Keith laughed. "Would you like somethin' to drink? Whatever you desire, we probably have it." He knew if his parents knew he was drinking they would have a fit, but he wasn't going to mess with their stash. He and his boys had their own private stash.

"I don't…" Mahogany started to say, but stopped herself. *What the hell?* she said to herself. "Yeah, but I'll leave it up to you. Whatever, you're drinkin', I'm drinkin'." She told herself that one drink wasn't gonna make her an alcoholic like her mother. Plus, she didn't want Keith to think she was a young and inexperienced teenager.

"Okay, boo, have a seat and feel free to turn on the stereo or television," Keith said, walking over to the bar.

I'm gon' get some of that today, he sang to himself. He poured them each of glass of Hypnotiq, which these days was the drink of choice for teenagers, and walked back over to where Mahogany was sitting on the sofa.

"Here you go, boo. Now go slow, that's some serious stuff."

"Thank you, but believe me, I can handle this," she said, even though she had no idea what she was about to drink. She took a small sip of the drink. She liked the sweet taste. It wasn't strong, like she thought it would be. "This tastes good. What is it?" she asked Keith.

"It's Hypnotiq," he said.

They sat back, drank a couple more glasses of Hypnotiq and

watched music videos on BET. Mahogany wasn't feeling any pain and she felt comfortable with Keith. She sat and told him about how lonely she was feeling at home, and how her mom was never there, and when she was she was drunk or sleep. He pretended to be interested in what she was saying, but he had other things on his mind.

He said, "Boo, I thought you wanted to come over here to get away from your troubles? Why did you bring them with you? You bringin' me down."

Slightly slurring, she said, "Baby, what can I do to make it up to you?"

"Well, you can come over here and let me taste those delicious looking lips of yours," he said. He pulled her into his arms, and started kissing her slowly at first, to test her reaction. Once he saw that she wasn't pushing him away, he went in for the kill.

As he was kissing her, he slipped his hand under her blouse and laid her back on the sofa.

Mahogany said, "Keith, we'd betta stop before your parents come home." She was afraid to tell him the real reason why she wanted him to stop. She knew if she told him she was a virgin, he'd drop her like a hot potato.

"Boo, don't worry about it, my parents aren't due home for a couple hours."

Okay, now how am I gonna get out of this one? "Well, they might come home early today," she said, trying to think of any excuse.

"Look, I got this, just relax," Keith said. "And don't worry, I have protection. I ain't tryna make no babies."

Well, at least he's thinking. That's probably because he has so many chicken heads, he's gotta think or he'd have plenty of baby mommas, Mahogany thought to herself.

Teenage Bluez II

* * *

About a half hour later, Mahogany came out the bathroom in Keith's basement, wondering how she had let things go that far. She told herself she would never drink again.

"Well, I have to be gettin' home, Keith." She couldn't look him in the face.

"Cool."

"So, are you gonna take me or do I have to take the bus?" she asked, since he didn't seem to be moving.

"I guess so," he said, getting up.

Once they pulled up in front of her house, before getting out the car, she said, "So, I guess I'll see you in school tomorrow."

She didn't know what else to say, because she was still feeling the effects of the Hynoptiq they had drank. And she was embarrassed about having sex with Keith. *Did we use a condom?* she asked herself, cause she couldn't remember. Now she had one more thing to worry about, whether she was pregnant or not.

"Boo, you know we will." Keith leaned over and kissed her on the lips. "And don't sweat tonight. I had fun. I hope we can do it again real soon."

Keith waited until Mahogany was safely inside before driving off. As he drove off, he was thinking, *Man, Mahogany is a real babe. I initially hooked up with her just to get in the panties, but after spending time with her, she's a'ight. I might have to make her my boo for real.*

Mahogany went inside to an empty house. This was one time she was glad her mom wasn't home, because she knew she would have gotten a beat down if her mom knew she had been drinking. No matter how much her mom drank, she never encouraged Mahogany to drink. As a matter of fact, she was the complete opposite, always warning her not to drink.

Mahogany went upstairs, got undressed and went to bed, forgetting all about calling Bianca.

When she got up the next morning, which was Friday, she was amazed she didn't have a hangover or anything. She still couldn't believe that she'd had sex with Keith. *Lord, please don't let me be pregnant,* she prayed, cause she still couldn't remember whether he wore a condom. *Darn, I can't let myself get into that situation again,* she told herself. *That was a stupid mistake.*

She went downstairs, and her mom was sitting at the kitchen table, drinking a cup of coffee, nursing a hangover. "So, what time did you get home?" she asked Mahogany.

"Not too late. I should be askin' you what time you got in, cause you wasn't home before I fell asleep," Mahogany said.

"Look, Mahogany, don't start with me this morning."

"What? I just asked you a question. I guess you're not feelin' too well again, huh?"

"Do you want some breakfast?"

"No, I'll get somethin' on my way to school. I guess I'll see you sometime this evening," Mahogany said, picking up her bag.

"I'ma be a little late tonight. One of the girl's on the job is getting married, and we're taking her out after work."

"Why doesn't that surprise me?"

"You know what, I'm sick of your attitude these days. You better remember who the mother is before you get hurt," Tanya said.

"Whatever, Mom. I'll see you whenever," Mahogany said, going out the door.

Once Mahogany got to school, she saw Bianca at her locker.

"Hey, girl," Mahogany said, walking up to her.

"Oh, now you wanna talk to me?" Bianca said, slamming her locker shut.

Mahogany saw that Bianca had an attitude, but couldn't figure out why. "What's wrong wit' you?"

"Why didn't you call me when you got home last night? I sat up half the night worrying 'bout you."

"Oh, snap! My bad, girl. Anyway, you should've called me if you were that worried."

"I didn't cause I was afraid your mom might've picked up. What do you think would've happened if I called and she answered and you wasn't home?"

"You right. Good lookin' out, girl."

"Well, how did it go last night?"

"It was real nice," Mahogany said, revealing nothing else. She had no intention of telling her about her night with Keith. She knew if she did, Bianca would have a fit, and she wasn't in the mood to hear a lecture. Right now, she wanted to hook up with Keith again, to find out where things stood with them.

At lunch, she saw Keith sitting at a table with some of his boys. "Hey, Keith," she said, walking up to the table.

"Hey, boo. What's good?" he said, walking over to her. "So how you feelin' today?"

"Fine, why?"

"Well, last night you wasn't feelin' any pain. You don't regret what happened, do you?"

"Naw, I'm cool," she said. She didn't want to ask him about last night, cause she was too embarrassed.

"So, how 'bout you give me your digits, so I can call you?" he asked.

"I was wondering why you didn't ask for them last night," Mahogany laughed. She gave him her number and they talked until Mahogany saw Bianca walk into the cafeteria. "Well, I betta go, Bianca's givin' me the evil eye. Hit me up later tonight," Mahogany said, walking away.

Bianca and Mahogany sat and ate lunch together. At the end

of the day, as they waited on the bus outside of Dobbins, Bianca asked Mahogany, "You want to come over for a while?"

"Naw, I'm gonna head on home. Maybe my mom will come home early and be sober, and we can spend some time together. Tomorrow we're supposed to hang out all day, but I'm not gonna hold my breath," Mahogany said sadly.

"Okay, well maybe we can hook up on Sunday and do somethin'," Bianca said.

The bus came, and they got on. Right before Bianca got off, she said, "Girl, I hope everything works out for you and your mom this weekend. Call me."

"Okay," Mahogany said.

A few stops later, she got off and walked up the sidewalk. Once she got in, she checked to see if her mother called, which she hadn't. So she changed her clothes, fixed herself something to eat, and went into the living room to watch television.

Around 4:30, Tanya called to remind her that she was going out after work, but that she would be home early. *Yeah right,* Mahogany said to herself.

About an hour later, her phone rang.

"Hello," she answered.

"Hey, boo. What ya doin'?" Keith said.

Hearing his voice brought a smile to her lips. "Nothin'. Just sittin' here watching *Hustle and Flow.*"

"Wanna hang out for a while?" he asked.

"I can't tonight. Me and my mom have plans to spend the weekend together. I'm waitin' for her to come home now. I've been lookin' forward to this all week. Can I get a rain check?" she asked, really hoping that she could.

"Sure, boo. How 'bout I call you on Sunday? Maybe we can go see a movie or somethin'."

"That sounds like a plan. Give me a call Sunday afternoon," Mahogany said.

"Cool. I'll talk to you then," Keith said.

Mahogany sat up waiting for her mother to come home. Around 10:00, she started getting pissed because she knew they wouldn't be spending Saturday together. More than likely, her mother would be nursing a hangover. She got up and went into the kitchen, with the intention of getting some water. Once she opened the cabinet, her mother's bottle of Seagram's vodka stood out, staring her in the face. She got a glass and decided to take a small drink.

After taking the first swallow of the vodka, her chest felt like it was about to explode. After the initial burning sensation passed, Mahogany downed the rest. She poured herself some more, this time she filled the glass halfway, and walked back into the living room. She sat there drinking and thinking about how messed up her life was.

An hour and two more glasses later, Mahogany had drunk over half the bottle. When she went to stand up, the room started spinning, and she felt nauseous. She stumbled upstairs, and was barely able to make it to the bathroom before she threw up. Once she emptied what was in her stomach, she crawled into her room, and fell into bed.

When Tanya finally made it home three hours later, she was drunk, and went straight to her room. She never bothered to peek in on Mahogany.

* * *

Around noon on Saturday, Tanya finally got up and yelled out, "Mahogany!" Hearing no response, she walked into Mahogany's room. "Girl, what are you doing still asleep? I thought we were gonna spend the day together?" When she got no response, she said, "Mahogany, do you hear me talking to you?"

She walked over to her daughter, who was laying on her stomach, and shook her. Mahogany didn't wake up. Tanya rolled her over onto her back. She smelled the alcohol on her daughter's breath.

"Girl, are you drunk?" Tanya said, shaking her again. When she saw that Mahogany wasn't waking up, she tried lifting her, and that's when she noticed she was totally unresponsive, and her body was cold and clammy. She took her in her arms, calling out her name.

"Mahogany, baby, wake up!" When she still didn't wake up, she lifted her eyelids, and she saw that her pupils were dilated. She immediately ran to the phone and dialed 911.

"Hello, what is your emergency?" the 911 operator said.

"I can't wake my daughter! She won't wake up!" Tanya yelled into the phone.

"Has she taken any drugs, Ma'am?"

"Not that I know of. But I think she's been drinking. I can smell it on her breath."

"Is she responsive at all?"

"No, and her skin is cold and clammy, and her pupils are dilated. Please help me!" Tanya yelled. "Please don't let my daughter die!" She gave the operator her address.

"Ma'am, calm down. An ambulance is being dispatched to your house. What I need you to do is turn her on her side, so if she vomits, she doesn't choke."

Tanya couldn't believe she was so busy wallowing in her own self-pity, that she didn't notice how much pain her daughter was in. She prayed, *Lord, I promise if You spare my daughter, I will go and get some help*.

About five minutes later, Tanya heard the sirens of the ambulance coming down the street. She ran downstairs and opened the door.

"She's upstairs," she said to the EMTs, as they entered her

home.

The EMTs went upstairs, checked Mahogany's vitals before putting her onto the stretcher. Then they whisked her away to the hospital.

Mahogany was in the hospital for a day before being released. After that, she and her mother went to counseling to help them deal with their issues. Tanya also enrolled in an Alcoholic Anonymous Program.

Tanya felt that things had a good and bad ending. The bad part was that she had almost lost her daughter, and the good part was that she is no longer drinking. She now spends time with Mahogany, and Mahogany is back at school, and has brought her grade point average back up. Tanya realized that things could have turned out so much worse, but with counseling, and the Lord's help, they were able to get through things.

While in counseling, the counselor suggested to Mahogany that she go visit her father. She stated to her that was the only way she would be able to deal with her feelings. She needed to let her father know how she felt about what he did to their family.

The following Saturday, Mahogany and her mother made the trip to the House of Corrections on State Road to visit Donte. Upon entering, Mahogany was taken aback by the strip search she had to endure. At that point, she was ready to turn around and go back home, but she knew she had to go through with this in order to heal.

They were then led into a waiting room, which was filled with other people waiting to visit inmates. She looked around at all the small children there, and wondered how someone could bring children that small to a place like this. After waiting about ten minutes, she saw her father walk through the door in his prison uniform. Immediately, all of the anger she had towards him came flooding back.

He walked over to them, kissed Tanya and tried to hug Mahogany, who pushed him away. He knew he couldn't get mad at her, but he was determined before they left, he would try and make up for all the pain he had caused her.

After they were seated, Donte said, "Mahogany, I know you're really upset with me. And I will apologize over and over again for all the pain I've caused you and your mom. I know what I did was wrong, but at the time I thought it wouldn't reach y'all."

"Come on, Dad. How could you even think somethin' like that? What, did you think you were beyond gettin' caught? Do you know what your being locked up has done to our family?" Mahogany stopped talking because she knew if she said anything else, she was gonna break down.

"Baby, I know what I did was wrong, and once I do my time, I will do anything in my power to make up for it. That I promise you." He hated to see the pain in his daughter's eyes.

"Daddy, I need you so bad. Do you know I almost died of alcohol poisoning because of you and mommy? And mommy was drinking so much that she never paid me any mind. I'm only sixteen, I need my parents to guide me into adulthood!" Mahogany got up from the table and walked over to the window.

During this time, Tanya was just sitting at the table with tears streaming down her face, saying nothing. She knew that Mahogany had to get all of this out of her system in order to heal. This was something Donte and Mahogany had to deal with one-on-one.

Donte got up from the table, and walked over to where Mahogany was standing. "Sweetie, please look at me," he said, turning her around to face him. "If I could take back that day, you know I would. But since I can't, all I can do is pray that one day you will forgive me."

"Daddy, I love you so much, but the day I saw you get

handcuffed and taken away in that police car was the worse day of my life. I miss you every single day. And yes, with time, I know that I will be able to forgive you. Do you realize that by the time you get out, I will be an adult? I will be twenty-three. You're gonna miss my high school graduation, my prom, all those important events in my life. These are things we can't get back. But let me ask you something, was it worth it?" She looked her father in the eyes.

"No, sweetie, it wasn't, and this is something I will have to live with for the next seven years. But I can promise you this, once I get out I will never deal drugs again. I will work at McDonald's first, flipping burgers, before I try and make quick money again. I've missed a part of your life that I will never be able to get back, and that's something I will regret the rest of my life," he said, with tears in his eyes.

Mahogany fell into her father's arms, and cried tears that she had held in for many years. They stood there for about ten minutes hugging and crying.

Before they knew it, visiting hours were over. Mahogany promised her father that she would be back to visit him again real soon.

And after that day, she stuck to that promise. Mahogany would go visit her father at least twice a month. Even though he still has seven years left on his sentence, Mahogany no longer feels like she is all alone, because she has her mother and father back in her life.

Keith and Mahogany are still seeing each other, but now they are no longer drinking or having sex.

Teenage Bluez II

HIS GRACE
by Marjani H.A. Aladin

"Diana Lee Cooper!" my father, James Warren Cooper, bellowed into the intercom from the basement of our three-story house. My father was a corporate lawyer, and one of the best. He was a partner at one of the largest firms in New Jersey. He loved spoiling himself with the most expensive and lavish items he could find.

I love our house. The sassiness of the Spanish style exterior perfectly compliments the sophisticated interior, which is filled with big screen plasma televisions, priceless pieces of art, including my father's prize Monet, and the most expensive foreign and antique furniture. When my friends come over, I see the jealousy plainly expressed on their faces as they enter the foyer with marble flooring, and a chandelier that takes their breath away. Many times, I find myself staring at the ceiling, admiring the hand carved angels that are intricately designed as a border, adding the finishing touch to each of the already exquisite rooms.

"Yes, Dad," I said cheerfully, from the top of the basement steps.

I didn't dare go down there, because ever since I was younger, I had been forbidden to enter his sanctuary. I never understood why the basement was so forbidden, but it was the rule, and I abided by it. The door always stood taunting me throughout my childhood. It was sealed with a padlock that secured my inability to gain access into the forbidden area. Once, when I was ten years old, one of my father's secret deliveries sat in the living room. The oddly shaped figure stood no taller than the top of my head. It was covered by an off-white tarp, which only increased my curiosity.

At that time, my father was dating a waitress he had met after a business meeting at a restaurant. I hated her, I hated all his girlfriends because they got the hugs I never got, and the attention I always wanted. One day when she came over, she made the mistake of uncovering a sheeted package. My father not only stopped her, but she left our home with bruises and welts, after he beat her like she was his child.

"Do you know how much that costs?" he screamed at her. "It's worth more than three of your lives! If something is covered in my home that means it's private! Stay out of my things. Everything I own is expensive, and you own and have nothing!"

I remembered that day like it was yesterday. After that, every time my curiosity rose, I resisted and walked away. I didn't want to be the next victim of my father's fit of rage.

"I'm going out tonight. A few of my clients are flying in from Tokyo and I'm taking them out for dinner. You're gonna have to make yourself something to eat," he said, into the intercom.

"Okay, Dad," I replied solemnly.

I wasn't sad because he was working and once again, I was left alone for a night. It was mainly because today was the first time in three weeks that my father and I were supposed to have dinner together. We had proclaimed it, *Family Fun Night*. This night had become of the utmost importance ever since he had agreed to it three weeks ago. It was a rare occasion that I got to spend time with him.

Teenage Bluez II

My emotions showed plainly on my face as I walked into my room. The wall-to-wall mirror that spread across the north side of my room only magnified the disappointment and hurt I was desperately trying to hide. As I looked in the mirror, I thought to myself, *Why won't he spend time with me? Do I look like my mother? Is that why it's hard for him to be around me?* As tears welled up in my eyes, I struggled to keep that first tear from falling, but my attempt was in vain. I sat in my room and cried softly. No sounds escaped, but warm salty tears rolled down my face, one after another, until there were no tears left to cry. I decided to go downstairs to talk to my father. I had to say something about my disappointment.

"Dad," I said nervously, from the top of the basement.

He mumbled an irritated, "Yeah."

"Umm…I just wanted to say I was really looking forward to tonight, and I…I…I, umm…" I stammered. I was nervous he would get mad at me and snap. Even though my father had never been abusive to me, I still lived in fear because I had seen his rage in action. "Umm…I was hoping we could maybe plan another day together soon." For the past two days, I had prayed he wouldn't forget about tonight, being how it was so important to me, but he did.

A disinterested grunt came from the basement. He didn't care, and I knew he didn't, so why did I care so much? Once again, warm tears started to roll down my already puffy and tear stained face. When I heard his heavy footsteps coming up the basement stairs, I quickly headed back to my room so he wouldn't see me. There was no good-bye or nothing, he just closed the front door, and once again, I was left in the house alone.

I often found myself planning extravagant and unrealistic events for a night with my father. Being that I don't have any siblings, and I haven't communicated with my mother in six years, having a relationship with my father was very important to me.

When I would tell my friends about my plans for a night with my dad, they would shake their heads disapprovingly. They thought it wasn't right that I had to literally schedule time to spend with my own father. I would tell them they just didn't understand.

Even though I was disappointed, I wasn't totally surprised. My father spent his time working or dating women who threw themselves at him because he was a good looking single man, with his career at the top and still rising. On days like this, I would find myself feeling empty, wishing I had a mother to fill the space my father wasn't filling.

My mother, Lillian Diane Cooper, and my father had gotten married six months into her pregnancy with me. At the time of my birth, my mother was seventeen, and my father was twenty-three. To those who looked at them from the outside, they were together for what seemed like a blissful nine years.

My mother was a quiet teenager, swept into marriage by the charm and good looks of an older man. Life seemed sweet because they would smile, and seemed to be madly in love when they thought people were looking. But I later learned their relationship wasn't as sweet as it seemed.

I remember the night my mother left us. I was only nine, and I heard screaming and yelling coming from the bottom of the stairs.

"You're not going anywhere, woman!" my father yelled at my mother.

I stayed hidden in the darkness of the staircase, watching my puffy eyed, crying mother yell back at my father. "You can't make me stay, James! I'm not seventeen anymore. I will not be your slave, and stop telling me what to do and what not to do! You don't control me!"

Teenage Bluez II

"You're nothing without me, Lil. You have nothing! No money and no place to stay. Sooner or later, you'll come crying back to me to forgive you."

I sat at the top of the steps, unable to move or scream because everything became a blur. I wanted so badly to run down the steps and into my mother's arms. The next day I found a letter she had left for me on my dresser. It read:

> *My Dearest Diana,*
> *I love you more than life itself. I know that you're a little too young to completely understand why Mommy had to leave you and Daddy. But when I was about sixteen years old, I met your father. He appeared to be the most charming, loving, sweet and affectionate man in the world. Unfortunately, I didn't know him as a person very well. So when we got married, I learned the hard way that your father and I just weren't good together. Just because I left, doesn't mean I don't love you. I love you more than anything, and I will come back for you. I know if I tried to take you now, both of our lives would be in danger because your father will not give you up without a fight.*
> *Also, I have no way to support you, and I don't want to put you through any hardship. But please believe that I will come back for you. I know your father will not let me talk to you if I call, so our communication will be limited for now. But no matter what, you're always in my heart. I love you.*
> *Love Always,*
> *Mommy*

So, for six years, I've had an absent mother and father, and I was getting used to it. I would often wonder why my mother never wrote me. At times, it would cross my mind that my father may have been hiding letters from my mother written to me. But I did not want to believe that he would go through all that trouble just to keep me away from the only mother I had, so I would push that thought out of my head whenever it crossed my mind.

*   *   *

That night, I ate a little bit of the food I had spent hours preparing for our *Family Fun Night*. After wrapping my father's plate carefully and neatly with foil, I placed it on the counter in plain sight so he could see it when he got home. Then it was TV, a bath, and getting my clothes out for school the next day. I fell asleep in the comfort of my Egyptian cotton sheets, on my king size canopy bed, wondering how different my life would be if I were a Cosby child, perfect in every way.

I woke up the next morning to an empty house. My father had gotten home last night after I was asleep, and left for work before I got up. Being home was miserable, because I was always so lonely. School was my life, not just the educational part, because I was an easy straight A student. The social part was my favorite.

As a freshman, I was living the high school dream. I was pretty and had the best looking friends, and could have any boy I wanted, but I didn't want any of them. It was really all about perfecting the art of flirting to me. It was a game, and I loved every second of it.

I couldn't blame the boys for wanting me; I was 5'5, with long black hair and a blessed bust and butt, which was topped off with the tightest stomach on a girl since Janet Jackson. Boys would always come to me, asking if they could come over. I'd smile sweetly, shrug my shoulders and walk away. I wasn't really going to have them come over, but high school was a play, nothing but an act, and I was the star. I worked the role I was given.

As I was at my locker, a soft deep voice whispered in my ear, "Yo, baby girl, what's good?" I knew who it was.

"Hey, handsome," I said, as I turned around.

Jamal Wright was my dream boy. He was a junior, and known by everyone who saw him walking down the hall. He was smart, a talented rapper, sweet, and to top it off, the most gorgeous creature I had ever seen. I wrapped my arms around him and melted as he squeezed me. This was our routine. Every time we saw each other, we hugged. Jamal wasn't my man, in fact, he was the only boy in school I wanted and couldn't have.

"How was your night last night?" I asked sweetly. We stood in the middle of the hallway, as if no one else was around.

"It was a'ight. I was chillin' with my brothers at the studio, working on the CD."

"Oh, okay," I said.

One of his boys came up to him and said, "What's up, Jamal?"

"Well, I see you have socializing to do," I said half-jokingly. "Call me later, okay."

"Yeah, okay," Jamal said. As I started to walk away, he called my name and gave me one last hug.

We had exchanged numbers a week after we met at the beginning of the school year. We loved our conversations at school, but wanted to talk more than the five minutes in between classes. Jamal and I had talked on the phone almost every day, until he got a girlfriend three weeks ago. But as I predicted, that relationship ended very quickly. Rumors said they broke up because his ex-girlfriend was a little too sexual for his taste. I had never heard of that being an issue with any other guy in high school before, but then again, Jamal wasn't any other guy. I must admit, even though I played no part in the separation with his ex, I was more than a little happy when he told me he was no longer in a relationship. I knew she wasn't what was best for him, because I thought I was. I was convinced he was supposed to be mine.

I walked away smiling, as the scent of Jamal lingered in my nose. I was snapped out of my daze by Tina, my best friend. We are tighter than Usher's six-pack. We tell each other everything. We met when we were in sixth grade, and in the three years we've known each other, our friendship has grown into something very special. Although our exteriors are different, we often think and react the same way in certain situations.

Tina was short, five feet at best, and a little on the chunky side. Her brown hair was usually pulled back into a neat ponytail, and unlike me, it was rare to see her in heels or dressed up. Her favorite attire was jeans and sneakers. Although we were close friends, I always felt a pull in our relationship when it came to guys, because I would often get more attention from them than her. But she was my girl through thick and thin.

"How was your family fun night, chick?" she said loudly. It amazed me how loud that girl could be at seven-thirty in the morning.

"Umm…"

"Girl, he canceled again, didn't he? I'm sorry." She paused for a second before quickly changing the subject. "Did you see Jamal today?" she asked, hoping to cheer me up.

"Yeah," I said coolly. It was so hard trying not to smile at the sound of his name. He made everything better.

After each of my ninety-minute classes, I would find myself rushing to opposite sides of the school just so I could walk past Jamal and get my hug, which was like a natural high. His hugs filled the spaces I was missing in my life. But every time he let go, the space seemed to get larger and larger.

"Earth to Diana!" Tina said, snapping me back to the present.

"Hey, girl, my bad," I said, with my mind still floating with thoughts of Jamal. "So, what's up?"

"Nothin', I'm ready to get outta here."

"Girl, we just got here, and you ready to leave," I laughed.

"Yeah. It seems like the day slows down when we're here, and speeds up while we're asleep," she replied.

"Yeah, I know what you mean. But we must get this knowledge."

"Whatever. Am I still comin' over your place today?"

"Yeah," I replied. "I'll catch up with you later. I gotta get to class."

Tina replied with a nod, as her eyes glided over the body of a boy walking down the hall. Tina was always looking at some boy. But I couldn't blame her this time, he was fine. His short cut hair perfectly complimented his green eyes and chocolate skin. He walked with a confidence that attracted attention. The way he dressed was well thought out. He looked as if he spent hours picking out his crisp white Roca-A-Wear tee with dark blue jeans, that drooped over his lower half, which was topped off with a fresh pair of white PF Air Forces. I walked away because I knew I had lost her to her new crush of the day.

After school, Tina met me at my locker and we went to my house to chill before she went home.

"D, can I raid your fridge?" she asked.

"Yeah, go ahead. Get me a soda too!" I yelled, from the living room.

Tina walked into the living room with her hands full of snacks. I got up to help her before she dropped something on our white carpet.

"Tina, what do you think about Jamal?" I asked her, after we were settled on the sofa.

"What do you mean? Besides the fact that you're head over heels in love with him and that's all you talk about? I really don't get you sometimes. You have mad guys all over you, tryna get with you and you're sweatin' Jamal. Why?"

"He's special, okay. He makes everything right."

Tina didn't understand why I felt the way I did about Jamal. I wanted him to be my boyfriend so bad because I liked him a lot. I was never the type to sweat a guy like that, so Tina just loved to poke fun at the one thing she knew rarely happened.

"Oh, whatever," she said jokingly, as she mouthed the word *sprung*. "Let's watch the movie." We had decided to watch *Coach Carter*, which I had picked up last week.

* * *

The next day I saw Jamal in the hallway. He looked so good. He had a fresh haircut and was wearing a white tee and jeans.

"Hey, handsome," I said shyly.

"Hey, what's up?" he said.

"Nothin'. I see you got your hair cut."

"Yeah," he replied. The expression on his face seemed shocked that I noticed, but I noticed everything about him.

"It looks good," I said smiling.

"Thanks." He gave me a hug and squeezed me extra tight. When he let go, I felt like Jell-O and floated to class.

A week passed before I finally got the nerve up to invite Jamal over to watch a movie. My dad wasn't going to be home, but he said it would be okay if Jamal came over. As I made the call, my heart was beating a million times a second. I was so nervous.

"Hello?" Jamal said, answering his phone.

"Hey, Jamal," I said, recognizing his voice. I had called him many times before, but never to ask him to come over.

"Hey, Diana. What's up?"

"Nothing. I was calling to see if you wanted to come over one day this week and chill wit' me?"

"You want me to come to your house?" he asked surprised.

"Yeah, if you want to. You don't have to if…" He cut me off.

"Yeah. I don't mind coming through to chill wit' you. How about tomorrow?"

"Yeah, that's cool," I said, trying to sound as relaxed as possible.

That night, I went to sleep with a smile so big on my face that my cheeks were hurting when I woke up the next morning.

The next day after school, I rushed home to prepare for Jamal's visit. When I walked into the living room, I found my father on the sofa. His shirt was half buttoned, his tie loose, and his normal perfect posture was replaced with a slump. I noticed a half empty bottle of scotch on the coffee table, but there was no glass. I dismissed the feeling that something was off, and started thinking about what I was going to say to Jamal when he arrived. After straightening up the already cleaned house, I prepared chips, dip, soda, candy, and any other treats I thought he might enjoy.

I then went to my room to change my clothes and do my hair. As I was going through my closet with just my underwear on, trying to decide on an outfit, my father came into my room with just his boxers on. I couldn't understand why he had gotten undressed, especially since he wasn't supposed to be home. He also never came into my room, so I became worried that something was wrong. He began talking slowly and softly, something I had seen him do many times before when he had one of his women over.

"Diana, you've grown into a beautifully developed young woman, just as beautiful as your mother was." I thought he was going to give me the sex talk because Jamal was coming over.

"I know I haven't paid much attention to you, sweetheart, but I'll try to do better."

He sat down on the bed and slowly stroked my face. It was awkward because it seemed like he was hitting on me, but I pushed that idea out of my mind. As he leaned in closer to me, I could smell the scotch on his breath. He was drunk!

In an instant, my father was on top of me, straddling me as he held my hands above my head with one hand, and trying to take off my underwear with the other. The smell of scotch, mixed with the smell of his aftershave, made me nauseous. I quickly realized my father was trying to rape me.

"Get off me! Get off!" Panic swept through my body. I locked my knees together so he couldn't enter me as I screamed for help. "Help…anyone, help me please!" I managed to choke out the words as tears rolled down my face. "Dad, why are you doing this to me? Someone help me! Stop, stop! Stop it!" I started gasping for air. The combination of the fear I was feeling, and the energy I was using to fight him off, started to make me dizzy.

He looked in my eyes quickly. The rage and hunger in his gaze scared me because I had seen that look in his eyes before. Whenever he wanted control over something he knew he couldn't have, he got that wild look in his eyes. Usually, whatever he was chasing wasn't really important to him, but it was the control that he lived for. My father would never let anything stop him from getting what he wanted, and that's what scared me.

"Dad, why are you doing this to me? Why?" I screamed again, hoping to bring him to his senses.

"Your mother left me!" he said. I could hear the mixture of pain and rage in his voice. "She left me with you! All these years I've had to deal with you, but look at you now…" His voice trailed off, as his sardonic tone hung thickly in the air.

"You're just as beautiful as she was. Tonight, I get my pay back for her…" he paused "…leaving you with me."

He loosened his grip on my hands, and I began hitting and scratching his face. I tried to slip from under him, but he quickly tightened his grasp and continued trying to pry open my locked legs. I tried with all my being to move him off me, but it was useless. My father worked out a lot and was much stronger than me.

Time seemed to slow down in the room — seconds turned into minutes, and minutes turned into hours. I felt as if I was being tortured forever. As I tried to regain my breath, I looked in my father's face, which was drained of any emotion. His eyes were filled with a look that could only be described as determination and concentration. He never looked regretful or mad. He didn't even seem to be enjoying himself, he was just concentrating on the task at hand, and I was determined not to let him succeed.

I continued trying to fight him off, but it only seemed to increase the force he was using on me. I continued to scream, but I knew no one would hear me because we were in the house alone. We didn't even have neighbors, because when my father had this house built, he isolated it from others. He said he wanted the privacy, so we never had close neighbors.

He was finally able to pry open my locked legs, long enough for him to make his move. Pain rushed up my body and through my spine. I had never felt any pain as intense as this before. Tears quickly rolled down my face, but I couldn't scream anymore. I thought I was going to pass out from his penetration, and his long back and forth movements only increased the severity of my pain. I couldn't understand why girls were so in love with sex. It hurt so much. Soon I became too weak to fight him anymore, and lay there crying until he was finished.

When he was done, he just walked out my bedroom and left the house. I turned over on my side and cried. I was so confused because I couldn't understand what had possessed my father to rape me. He had never came on to me before, tried to feel on me, or anything. I laid on my bed in shock. My body was so numb from the pain I had just experienced, that my emotions didn't register. *I need to call the cops,* I thought to myself.

Ten minutes later, I heard the doorbell ring. I ignored it. "Brrrrrrrrrrring" it rang again. Slowly I pried myself from my bed, and looked out the window that overlooked the front of our house. It was Jamal. I had forgotten he was coming over. Suddenly I broke down. I couldn't handle being around him right now. I dragged myself down the steps so I could cancel our plans. I found it almost close to impossible to move, my body felt like it was in shock, and the pain heightened with every breath.

"Diana!" Jamal yelled, through the closed front door.

"Yeah," I whispered, as I opened the door. He walked in. I wanted to protest his entry, but was just too weak.

His face glowed in admiration at the size of my house, but as he turned to face me, his sunny disposition quickly faded. It was replaced with concern as he looked at my torn clothing, tear streaked face, and how I was shaking uncontrollably. I tried to hold back the tears, but they welled up quickly and poured out the corners of my swollen eyes.

"What happened? What's wrong?" he asked hesitantly.

I shook my head. Not only could I not involve him in something like this, but I didn't know if I could even actually formulate into words what happened. I still couldn't believe it myself. Everything was a blur, one horrible unforgettable blur.

"Diana, you have to tell me what's wrong. Whatever it is, I'm sure I can help."

"No," I said quietly, "you just don't understand."

"Tell me so I can help you," he said softly, as he gently wiped the tear that ran down my left cheek. I looked at him and saw the sincerity in his eyes. Knowing that he cared only added to my emotional pot of soup and I broke down.

After an hour of sobbing and trying to get my story out, Jamal finally understood what happened. His face turned from confusion to shear terror and shock. Then I saw anger, mixed with deep sadness, stir in him.

"Have you called the police yet? Where's your father? We're leaving now!" he managed to say in one quick breath.

"W…W…What! Umm, well no, I didn't call the police. I don't know if I will, and…" He cut me off.

His voice was full of anger. "Diana, you don't have a choice. You can't let your father get away with this. You *have* to go to the police. I'm not gonna let you stay here. Now, get your shoes on!" he said, walking to the front door.

I sat there shocked and confused. I was filled with mixed emotions. I knew Jamal was right, but how could I send my own father to jail? If I did, I would have no family left, and I'd be alone.

"Now!" he repeated, interrupting my thoughts.

"Okay, just let me take a shower and get changed. I feel so disgusting," I whined.

He seemed to contemplate my statement, before rejecting it. "You can't take a shower, the police will need to gather evidence. Now, let's go!"

"Okay," I said reluctantly.

On the drive to the police station, I was silent, but every so often Jamal would squeeze my hand, as if reassuring me I was doing the right thing.

As we pulled up to the police station, I looked at Jamal with pure fear in my eyes. He nodded as if he understood. I kept wondering how he could be so levelheaded in this situation.

Why did he care so much? When he came in my house, he could have ignored his instincts that something was wrong and left, but he didn't. My thoughts trailed off as I wondered if I was doing the right thing.

"I'm not sure if I should do this," I told Jamal, totally scared out my mind.

"Of course you should. I know he's your father, but he raped you. He had no right to take advantage of you and violate you like that." He was starting to get upset again. "We're going inside, and you're gonna make a report."

"But if I do this, I'll have nothing, no one. I have no place to go, no family to go to. What will I do? I can't go back home. I'm stuck."

"No, you're not." He paused. "You have me. If you can't stay with Tina, you can stay with me. My parents won't mind. Now, we have to go in."

I felt safe with him. But I was still shaken because the perfection of my little world had just been shattered, and I had no idea how, why, or even how to fix it. But it seemed as if Jamal did know how to fix it, how to make everything right.

We walked into the station. "How may I help you?" the officer at the front desk asked.

"I…I…umm," I stammered. I couldn't get the words out.

"She's here to report a rape. Her father raped her," Jamal said sternly. It seemed as if the whole station came to a halt when he said those words. The officer took my name, age, my father's name, and other information before getting on the phone.

As I sat waiting, a woman with a black afro came up to me. "Hello, Diana. I'm Elisa Thompson, and I'm from the Special Victims Unit. We deal with rape victims such as yourself. Because you're under the age of eighteen, I will be accompanying you throughout this time, and helping you with any problems or questions you may have."

"Okay," I whispered. I was still frightened, but hearing Ms. Thompson say she would be with me throughout, made me feel a little safer.

As she spoke, the word *victim* circled in my mind. Was I really the victim? Or had I been the catalyst to this horrible event? Had all my pajama shorts been too short? Did I seduce him? No! Everyone was saying I was the victim.

I looked over at Jamal, he was talking on the phone. My attention suddenly shifted from my thoughts of the part I played in this horrific incident, to the conversation Jamal was having. A grim expression was spread across his face as he talked in a hushed tone. His expression showed nervousness, and I could tell the strong and calm composure he held earlier was just a mere façade. He was just as nervous and scared as I was. I immediately regretted bringing him into this drama.

I wasn't able to hear the conversation, although I tried my hardest. It seemed like everything in the station roared with noise the more I tried to listen. A few minutes later, Jamal walked back over to me, with his normal face of cool strength and composure.

"Tina and her mom are on their way…" His voice trailed off.

"You called Tina and her mother?" my voiced cracked with embarrassment.

"Well, it wasn't my idea," he said. It seemed as if he read my thoughts. "The lady from SVU asked if I knew of any other family you could call, since you have to have a legal guardian responsible for you. I hope you don't mind." His eyes continuously searched the room, as if the words he wanted to say were somehow bound in the paint on the walls.

"We'll be leaving for the hospital in a few minutes. Okay?" Mrs. Thompson said reassuringly, walking back over to me. The cool soft tone of her voice was comforting to my ears. As she talked, I felt my muscles relax. I had a strong need to hug her.

I responded with a slight nod. As Mrs. Thompson and I were escorted to a standard black and white police car by a tall gangly looking police officer with olive skin and a strong Italian accent. When we arrived at Jacob Memorial Hospital, I dragged myself to the examination room, where a pretty Puerto Rican doctor sat, already prepared for my arrival. She introduced herself as Dr. Diaz.

"Diana Cooper, I presume?" she asked, with a sympathetic smile.

I didn't answer, but sat silently on the table instead. I wasn't sure what exactly was going to happen, because although Mrs. Thompson had briefly gone over the details of the examination, my mind was still in a fog of emotions.

"Diana, I know this is a difficult time for you, so I'll try to be as quick as possible. Your guardian will be with us in a moment."

I sat there stunned. A few minutes later, Tina's mother came busting into the room. Tears of concern ran down her face as she hugged me and asked me a million questions. She told me she was going to be my legal guardian until further notice.

"Oh, goodness! Diana, are you okay sweetheart?" Tina's mother cried, as she swept me into her motherly arms. Being wrapped in her arms was like being wrapped in a warm marshmallow. I merely nodded as a response to her question. "Oh, when I think what that horrible man did to you. You know, I never really liked him. Oh, goodness," she rambled on, in an exasperated tone.

"I'm fine, really I am," I said, in a pathetic attempt at sounding cheerful.

"Oh, of course you're not okay," she said, as her bottom lip quivered. Her now dry tear streaked face was once again flooded as her eyes welled up with tears. She cupped my hand lovingly, and my body flooded with warmth as my desire for a mother filled my heart.

The doctor asked if I wanted Tina's mother in the room during the examination. I responded no, and she was escorted out to complete some paperwork. Mrs. Thompson assured Tina's mother that she would be in the room with me during the examination.

"Diana, I'm going to leave the room so you can get undressed. Put this hospital gown on and I'll be right back," Dr. Diaz said. By the time I was done putting on the gown, she had returned. "Okay, what I have to do now is check you out so we can find out if you've been damaged in any way during the rape. We also have to do tests to find out if you've contracted any sexually transmitted diseases. In a week, you can come back, and at that time, we'll do a pregnancy test. This may be a little uncomfortable, but it's necessary. I'll try to make it as quick as possible. Please lie on your back, spread your legs and bend them. Try to relax."

"Umm…can I ask you a question?" I asked the doctor nervously.

"Of course."

"I've maintained my virginity for fifteen years and now it has been stolen. What does that mean? Losing my virginity was one of the worst experiences in my life. It was my pride and joy. And after today, my life will definitely be changed forever."

"Well, that's a very good question. You're physically not a virgin, but since you didn't make the decision as an individual to have sex, that makes you very spiritual. Do you understand?"

"Yes, but what if I have a disease, or I'm pregnant? What will happen to me then?"

"If you've contracted an STD, you will have medicine you will have to take. There are some diseases we can just give you medicine for and it will be gone. Unfortunately, if you've contracted HIV, we can't cure that. There's medication that you can take that will extend your lifespan, but none that cure the virus. If you're pregnant, then you have quite a few decisions to make. You can choose to abort the baby, you can carry the baby to full term and give it up for adoption, or you can keep your child."

"I understand," I said quietly.

"Anything else?" she asked. I shook my head no in response and began to lie down as she had previously instructed.

Relaxing was the last thing I was able to do. I was completely exposed to some woman I didn't even know. Suddenly, I felt a startling coldness in between my legs. As it entered me, a throbbing pain swept through my body as it stretched my insides. As I struggled to relax in spite of the pain, I heard Dr. Diaz say she was going to collect some of my father's DNA from inside of me. I felt a cotton-like material sweep across my insides. Finally, she took the metal object out of me, and my body relaxed. After the examination, I was driven back to the police station, but this time it was by Tina's mother.

"How are you feeling, dear?" she asked, as she drove.

"I'm fine," I lied. The truth was I didn't know how I felt. I hadn't had a chance to sort out my emotions. Everything was happening so fast.

When we got back to the police station, I was taken into a room with Detective Holzer and Tina's mother. Tina and Jamal went to get something to eat while they waited.

"Ms. Cooper, I know this is a very difficult time for you, but I have to know exactly what happened tonight. Okay?" I nodded slowly. I looked the detective over. He was a small, portly man with little short fingers and a bushy cowboy type mustache. "I must also tell you that anything you tell us will be held in a court of law, and it's against the law to lie in these circumstances. I understand it was your father who raped you tonight, am I correct?"

"Yes sir," I said nervously.

"And besides your friend's mother, you have no other legal guardian or family that you know of, also correct?"

"Yes, sir. I haven't seen or had contact with my mother since I was nine years old," I said.

"Okay. Well, because you have no legal guardian, and you're a minor, we must let you know that we have assigned your friend's mother as your legal guardian until further notice. Just for now, until we can help you find your mother. Okay?"

I didn't respond. Where were they going to find my mother? I didn't even think she was still alive. But what if she was, and what if they found her, then what?

"Okay. Well, why don't you start by telling me what happened, and I'm gonna write down what you tell me. This will be your written statement of the events that occurred today that we will take to court," Captain Holzer said.

"Well, earlier today I came home and started cleaning up because my friend, Jamal, was supposed be coming over to hang out with me today."

"Is this boy your boyfriend?"

"No, sir, just a friend."

"Okay, continue."

"While I was getting dressed, my father came into my room, which startled me because he never comes into my room. Then he started talking to me as if he was trying to seduce me."

"Had he ever talked to you like that before, or shown any other form of inappropriate behavior towards you?"

"No, sir. My father is hardly ever home, and when he is, he doesn't pay me any attention. That's why, when he came into my room, I became worried that something was wrong. And I think he was drunk."

"Why would you think that?"

"I could smell the alcohol on his breath when he was…" I paused. "…on top of me."

"Okay, continue."

"He told me that I had developed into a beautiful young lady, and then he jumped on me and started to force himself on me. He was very aggressive. He pulled and yanked at my clothes. I tried to fight him off. I kicked and screamed and asked him why he was doing this to me. He never answered." Tears started streaming down my face. "He never said a word. He had such a crazed, hungry look in his eyes, like a wild hungry animal chasing after his prey. He just got up and left when it was over. Then I just lay there. I was so confused, hurt and shocked, that my first thought wasn't to call the police. Then the door bell rang and it was Jamal. When I answered the door, I was going to tell him that we had to cancel until another day. But he saw that something was wrong, and I ended up breaking down and telling him what happened." I paused, as I tried to catch my breath through my crying. The detective passed me some tissues.

"Then what happened?" he asked.

"Jamal convinced me to go to the police. I wasn't going to go because I don't have any family, and if my father were arrested, I'd be an orphan. But he said that I had to. Then he drove me to the police station. He's still outside waiting."

After Captain Holzer repeated everything I told him, he had me read over what he wrote to make sure it was correct, and sign it at the bottom to verify that I said all of what was written down. Then a lady came in with two charts, one of a man and one of a woman. She asked me to circle all the parts he touched on my body with his body.

When everything was completely finished, we started to leave the police station. As we exited the building, we passed two cops who had my father in handcuffs. They had arrested him at his office. I'm sure that was embarrassing for him, because he was probably in an important meeting. As they passed, fear and guilt flowed through my body. His eyes locked with mine, as I searched for any kind of emotion in the deep brown of his eyes. I found nothing but anger. Once again, fear crept through my body and my head started to throb as I noticed my hands shaking uncontrollably. I quickly looked away, hoping to never have to look in his eyes again.

"You're just like your mother…ungrateful. I gave you everything…everything. You owe me. You owe me…" his voice trailed off, as he was pulled down the hall by the officers that were struggling to keep my fighting father under control.

Since Tina's mother was now my guardian, I was going to stay with them until the Court could locate my mother. I had to get some clothes from my house, so a police officer escorted me inside. I went in and got my clothes. It felt weird to be back in my room.

On my way out, my eyes glanced over at the locked basement door. The need to see why my father spent so much time down there was overwhelming. My heart raced as I moved cautiously to the door. I knew my father wasn't down there, but the same fear from my childhood bubbled up inside of me. I found the door unlocked and edged my way along the dark stairway. When I reached the bottom step, I hit the light switch. There, I found a slew of electronics and games, TV's, computers, a pool table, and in the middle of the room sat a mahogany wooden desk.

I went to the desk, opened the drawer, and found it lined with letters and cards. They were all addressed to me, each and every one of them. There in front of me lay six years of letters and cards from my mother that I never got. My father had been hiding them from me. Anger swept over me as I grabbed all the letters and cards and put them carefully into my bag.

That night at Tina's house, I lay restlessly. I tossed and turned. It felt so weird to not be in my house, and to have someone in the house with me. I hoped they would find my mother, because I had so many things to say to her. I laid in bed reading the six years of letters and cards from my mother that my father had kept from me. Tears slowly ran down my face as I dozed off to sleep.

* * *

The next week, I went to the hospital to get my pregnancy test done. They told me I would receive a letter in the mail within a week with the results from the pregnancy test, and the information from the rape kit. Four days later, I received papers saying the rape kit had come back negative for any sexual diseases or severe damage, but it said I was pregnant.

"My stomach feels as if it dropped through the floor. Nothing could be worse than being pregnant by a father that raped you," I told Tina, as I cried in her arms. "I decided I'm going to abort the child. I don't want to be a teenage mother. I didn't make the decision to have sex!" I began to yell at her. "Why is this happening to me? It's not fair! I'm not going to live with the consequences of my father's actions. I have to abort this baby. I have to." I cried myself to sleep that night. I was so drained and upset. I didn't know why my life had changed so much so quickly.

I was sent to counseling, where we talked about the rape and how it made me feel. At first I shut down and refused to talk. How could I explain my feelings if I didn't know how I felt myself? At first, it was hard to open up because I had suppressed my feelings inside. I felt I had no one to run to, no one to talk to. I felt so dirty and guilty inside, even though I hadn't done anything wrong. It finally felt good to talk about it, but I only received full closure after Jamal started taking me to church with him. I became very close in my relationship with God.

After a month of staying with Tina, the Court decided I needed to find my mother. They found her through the computer database. They said it was easy to find her because she worked for a local newspaper in New Jersey. When they initially contacted my mother, she was hesitant, because after six years, she didn't know how I would react to her coming back into my life. But once they told her about me accusing my father of raping me, she knew she had to see me. My mother was overjoyed to have her daughter back, but I wasn't, because of all the anger I had suppressed.

We had to go to court in order for my mother to get custody of me. At first, I was going to fight it, and ask the court to allow me to stay with Tina and her mother, but once I saw my mother in court, all the love I had for her came flooding back, even though I was still angry at her for leaving me.

A month later when I moved in with her, my emotions were mixed. I was moving in with the one person I had longed to see after all these years. But I couldn't help but feel bitter because she got away from my father's abuse and left me to be his victim. If she hadn't left me, my father would not have ended up raping me. Even though I had missed out on a mother all these years, at least I had her now when I really needed her. I was happy, but also upset.

"Where have you been all these years?" I yelled bitterly at her. "Did you just forget that you had a daughter who was living in a house with no love? I didn't know if you were dead or alive, or just not thinking about me."

"Sweetheart…" she started. I cut her off. Her expression said that I had hurt her feelings. I knew she only had my best interest in mind when she left me with my father, but I was still hurt. The fact that she knew that she hurt me hurt her.

"Don't sweetheart me. I don't even know you. You've been gone all my life, and you think you can just walk right back in because Dad is gone. You're not the good guy, if that's what you're thinking! You abandoned me! Right now you're the lesser of two evils!" I yelled finally. I had tired myself out yelling at her.

"I'm so, so, sorry," my mother cried. I saw her strength weaken with every word. "I shouldn't have left you with that bastard. I hate him. I hate myself for leaving you with him. I'd give my soul to take it back, but I can't. He's the scum of the earth!" she yelled. My mother started crying. "I'm so sorry. I regret leaving you with that sorry excuse for a man." Anger was plastered on her face. "I love you. I was young, dumb and scared when I left your father, and was only trying to make sure you never lacked anything. That's why I left you, but I thought about you everyday," she said sincerely.

I knew she loved me and was sorry for leaving. I wanted to be mad, I wanted to hate my mom, but whom would I go to? She was all that I had left. After we made up, my anger had slightly subdued. Although, I was still upset that I hadn't seen her since I was nine. I wanted to know about her life. We knew nothing about each other.

"Sweetheart, you know I've missed you, right?"

"Yes, Mom. I've missed you too. What have you been doing these last six years?"

"I'm a writer. I write an advice column for young and abused mothers for a local newspaper. I don't want any other young girls to be physically, emotionally, or sexually abused by their husbands or boyfriends, as your father was to me and now you."

Teenage Bluez II

* * *

Everything in my life was going well after that. Three months later, I was still going to counseling, going to church, and my relationship with my mother was excellent.

"So, you really gonna abort the baby?" Tina asked one night, as we talked on the phone.

"Yes. I want to go to Planned Parenthood, but I'm afraid to alone. I know my mom will go with me, but will you come too?"

"Of course I'll go with you. I have to say I don't approve, but if I were in your shoes, I don't know what I'd do, so I'm not gonna judge you. When do you want to go?"

"Is next Thursday good?" I asked. I could see my mother breaking into tears out the corner of my eye. She didn't approve either, but told me it was my choice.

"Yeah, I'll be there," Tina said. We said our goodbyes and I went to sleep.

On Friday, I talked to Jamal and told him about my planned visit to Planned Pregnancy. That Sunday at church, Jamal told me he didn't think I should get the abortion. He also asked me to be his girlfriend. I was so thrilled. He wanted to be with me, even though I had been raped and was pregnant. He saw me when I wasn't the cutest, and still wanted to be with me. I jokingly told Tina I thought I was in love.

The night before I was to go to Planned Parenthood, Jamal prayed with me over the phone. He said if I wasn't sure what I wanted to do with the baby, that I should ask God. After hanging up with him, I got on my knees and prayed to God for a sign.

"Lord, if I'm supposed to keep this baby, please give me a sign. I don't know what to do. I need Your help. How can I keep a baby that my father will be the daddy and grandfather to?" As

I was praying, a bright light suddenly came through my window, and I knew what I had to do.

I woke up on Thursday morning, and never went to my appointment at Planned Parenthood. I had made the decision to keep my child. I knew that it was going to be a hard road, and that it would take up a lot of the time I would have as a normal teenager, but it was better than dealing with the guilt of aborting my baby.

It was hard to raise a child, but I had help. My mother, Tina and Jamal helped me take care of my beautiful baby boy, Joseph Tyler Wright. I gave Joseph Jamal's last name because he became my fiancé two weeks before Joseph was born.

About three months later, my father's trial took place. He pleaded "not guilty" to the charge of raping me. The evidence was overwhelmingly against him, so the judge sentenced him to twenty years to life in prison. I never saw my father after the day of the trial. Testifying against him was strenuous, but I gave the same statement I gave at the police station the night of the rape. My nightmare was finally over.

My mother went to the sentencing for me. She took poems and my diary that proved I had been emotionally and physically affected. The birth of my son was also evidence, because he had my father's DNA. That day, my mother was escorted out of the courtroom because she broke into a fit of rage when she saw him.

"You're a jerk! I can't believe you would do this to our daughter! You pig!" she shouted, as she spit in his face. "You disgust me. I hope you rot in jail for what you've done!" Her words were a mixture of her anger and mine. After the trial, I wasn't upset, and after my mother said her words to my father, neither was she. Life went on by the grace of God.

When Jamal got out of high school, we got married. Going to school, working, and taking care of a baby were hard. But with God's grace and love, I made it through. God helped me realize I was a victim, but my baby wasn't the enemy, and I love him and my husband so much.

Tina became the Godmother for my child and the bridesmaid at my wedding. My mother and I grew closer each day. I still had some resentment toward her, but every day, with God's grace, I was working through it.

My father died after his sixth months in jail. He apparently tried to control some of the guys in jail, by telling them they had to listen and follow him because he was smarter than they were. Those guys weren't as easy to control as I was, and they got together and jumped him. He was in the hospital for two weeks before he died from massive blood loss and severe trauma to the head.

His Will was settled and read two weeks later. The house was left to me, and it's the house that Jamal and I now raise our precious son in. Jamal and I continued going to church together and we grew in our faith. Many times I found myself wondering if I could deal with the demons of my past. They had become a roadblock that I couldn't overcome alone. As I was praying on night, God spoke to me. He told me to turn to Philippians 4: 13.

It reads: *I can do all things through Christ who strengthens me*. Thank God, He gave me grace and the strength to go on.

Teenage Bluez II

CONFUSED
by Kinae Kelly

I hopped out of bed in a hurry, excited about my second day of school. I had laid out the finest clothes in my closet the night before, making sure I would be dressed to impress when I hit the doors of Drew Hill High. Today would be our first after school activity, and my first opportunity to check out the older fellas. I had seen a few cuties yesterday, and had my eye on one or two football players, but nobody special.

Glancing at the clock, I quickly showered and slipped on my cropped neck DKNY shirt and snatched my new Baby Phat jeans off the bed. I tried to put them on in a hurry, but as they reached my thighs, I twisted and turned, struggling to pull them up. They were a size four, which caused my size seven body to scream as I tried to squeeze into the tiny pair of jeans.

It was important for my outfit to be just right, because it was the only way to win me some brownie points with the guys. In high school everybody judges you on what you wear and who you hang out with. Both my aunt and friends had always said I was a cutie, but I didn't agree. So I figured my looks wouldn't get me too far, therefore my gear had to be right. At average height, my shape was coming along slowly. I wasn't fully developed and busty like the other girls, and my butt was far from being big and bootylicious.

The moment I finally got the zipper up, I exhaled. I smiled

in the mirror, happy about the way I looked. My jeans were so tight I was barely able to bend over to lift my book bag from off the floor.

I hated carrying the plain book bag my aunt had gotten me. I learned quickly that it wasn't cool to be seen carrying books the first few days of high school. As a freshman, people had told me high school would be nothing like junior high, but I never understood what they meant until now.

At fifteen, I was already dying to hang out with the most popular girls and wear name brand clothes, clothes I couldn't really afford. But I was willing to flip burgers, sew baskets, and sweep streets if I had to.

Unfortunately for me, my mother dropped me off on my aunt's doorstep six years ago so she could run the streets as she pleased, so I didn't have much money. My Aunt Laurie and I have been struggling since that day, and nothing seems to be changing. We're broke, broke, broke! I just make the best of it, and pray as often as I can. Just like now, I definitely need to pray for these out-dated shoes.

I took a minute to look down at my tinted Reeboks and wondered when things would change for us. My Aunt Laurie was up for a promotion at her job, and was hoping to bring more money into the house soon. But it was obvious she didn't let our disadvantages or hardships in life get her down. Most days, she walks around humming spirituals, and smiling like she has just won the lottery.

Today, Aunt Laurie was really off the hook. I could hear her in the kitchen, chanting and singing like she was part of a Mass Choir. I knew once I tried to sneak pass her in my tight jeans, she was gonna point her finger to the back of our small apartment, sending me back to my room to change. If I didn't know any better, I'd think she got drunk daily. She always behaved wildly, with a sarcastic mouth, yet she was a devout

Christian. At times, she'd curse me out, and then quote me a scripture immediately afterwards.

She would always preach to me. "Shawna," she'd say. "I know I get crazy sometimes, but I gotta keep your lil' butt in check. You got the potential to be fast. So, if I say something not too Christian-like, forgive me. I never said I was perfect, chile. I'm a work in progress, and trust me, I do love the Lord."

I knew my Aunt Laurie like the back of my hand, and her words stayed embedded in my mind. That's why I crept down the hall, headed to the door like a mental patient trying to escape from the crazy ward. Just as I opened the door slowly, the squeaky noise startled her.

She appeared out of nowhere. "Now, where in the world do you think you're going looking like a hoochie in training, chile? I know I raised you better than that!" Aunt Laurie stood with her hands on her hips and a dishtowel draped over her shoulder.

"I'm goin' to school," I responded, like I hadn't done anything wrong.

"Oh, so you wanna be a follower, huh?"

I didn't respond, 'cause I was nervous as I don't know what. Standing still, I froze near the door.

"Be not of this world," she said firmly. As she got closer, I just knew she was gonna haul off and hit me with the dish rag. She scanned me up and down, before struggling to grasp a patch of my jeans near my thigh. "You see that!" she screamed. "No room! They're too tight! Go take'em off!" She pointed toward the bedroom. "And stop trying to be like those fast girls up at that school!"

I was so pissed. By the time I changed and went through her rigorous inspection, I had missed my bus. Twenty minutes later, I found myself riding in the car with my aunt, headed toward school. She looked a mess, so I tried not to say much, just in case she wanted to continue the conversation once we got to the school. I mean, coming out of the house in a beat up sweatshirt was one thing, but the big pink rollers were straight humiliating.

"So, what's this mess you tryna stay after school for today?" she asked, breaking the silence.

"It's an afternoon club where different teachers come together to give students a chance to interact outside of the classroom," I answered, with worry in my voice. She had given me her approval the day before, but that meant nothing. I knew it wouldn't take much for her to change her mind.

"Now, tell me again who these girls are that you plan on walking home with? And are they in the club too?"

"Oh, God! Do I have to go through the third degree again?"

"Yes, you do. And don't be using the Lord's name in vain either. He died on the cross for your sins, so don't call him unless you need him. Now, give me their names."

"Lisa, Shenekwa, and a few other girls."

Aunt Laurie went crazy. "Shenekwa?" she asked. "First of all, she's seems way too advanced for you. And secondly, who would name their daughter, Shenekwa? And you think I want you hanging out with her?"

"Why would her name determine what type of person she is? When we go to church, our pastor teaches us to love everyone. Right?" I asked, with emotion. I knew if I mentioned church, I could calm her down. Besides, she knew Lisa very well, and knew her mother wasn't going for anything unholy either.

"You're right," she said, pulling up to the front of the school. "I shouldn't judge her based on her name. And, yes, the pastor does teach us that God loves us all. But He must've been sleeping when He let that girl's momma name her Shenekwa."

We looked at each other and laughed just as my girls walked past the car. They waved, but didn't stop, which was fine by me. Aunt Laurie had a ruthless reputation of putting young girls on the spot. If you spoke out of line, looked like you were doing something wrong, or even smiled the wrong way, she'd check you. Like scared cubs, my girls gathered at the front door of the school and motioned for me to join them.

I hopped out of the car like an escapee, hearing my aunt yell, "Be home by five o'clock, or that'll be the last after school activity you attend!"

Embarrassed, I jetted to the front, joined the huddle, and hugged my girls like we hadn't seen each other in days. Lisa and Shanekwa were both considered my best friends, but I couldn't help but frown inside at Shanekwa's wild outfit.

Yeah, she was a sophomore, and had already built a reputation as a good dresser, but I was really disappointed in her outfit. She was rocked out in crazy colors from head to toe, like she was a runway model setting new trends. As the tallest of us all, her long legs were covered in knee-length, checkered socks that reached almost to her gauchos. I stared at her multi-colored shirt that fit tightly across her chest, showing off her big boobs. I tried my best not to make any faces. However, it must have showed, 'cause she gritted on me like I was the enemy.

"You like the outfit," she teased, catching my stare. Shanekwa turned from side to side, so that I could be jealous of every stitch.

It wasn't right for me to tell her that I thought she was colorblind. Besides, she would've thought I was hating anyway, 'cause everybody considered her the best dressed girl in school. In my opinion, she was just a strange dresser pretending to be up on the latest international fashions. Thank goodness she was my friend, or I would have plenty of jokes.

"Nah, I don't like it, I love it," I said, slapping Lisa's hand high in the air. We both looked at each other like, *yeah right, we're lying our butts off*.

Now Lisa, I loved her because she was so down to earth, and

a normal dresser. She acted more like me and looked like me too. Lisa had on a short jean dress, with a wide silver belt and a pair of low heel mules. She knew I was checking her out, 'cause that's what we did every morning. But we looked at each other with a funny expression as our eyes met each other's head.

"Nice hair style," she joked, complimenting me on my long, press and curl job.

"Yeah, you too," I laughed. "You just got hit with a lil' too much grease."

She yanked the mess out of my hair. "You shouldn't wanna be like me," she joked.

We knew when my aunt and her mother had sent us to the same hairdresser over the weekend, we were gonna look like twins. We didn't care. We loved it. Shanekwa was the one who wanted to be Miss Individuality. Unfortunately for her, her micro-braids looked like they were coming up on an anniversary and needed re-braiding as soon as possible.

Our fun, chill time ended when Mr. Evans, one of our security administrators, brushed us inside the last set of double doors and down the hall. His walkie-talkie sounded with all of the commotion coming from other areas in the building. At three minutes to eight, it didn't seem like he could get everyone inside their classrooms on time.

"That's enough," he said. "It's time to put something into those heads. When that bell rings at eight o'clock, anyone left in these halls is going with me." His deep voice echoed through the hall.

I looked at him, wanting to call him corny straight to his face. Then I decided against it and moved along. Spending the second day of school in detention wouldn't be too cool. As soon as we got to the bottom of the staircase, Shanekwa shot us instructions on where to meet her after first period and gave us a sexy-like wave goodbye. *She was so dramatic, even so early in the morning*, I thought.

Lisa and I glanced at our schedules, realizing that we both had science for our first period class. It was 'B' day, and our first day attending this particular class. The whole 'A' day 'B' day thing would take some getting used to. On 'A' days, I'd have to take one set of classes, and then on 'B' days, I'd take another set of classes. I shook my head at the thought of remembering which days were which.

Lisa grabbed me by the arm after noticing the time, and we rushed down the hall like we were running to catch a flight. Lisa stopped dead in her tracks to ask the sexiest guy I had seen in days if he knew where Room 101 was located.

"Isn't that a lab?" he asked.

"Beats me." She hunched her shoulders and gave him an innocent look.

She wasn't slick. I thought he was a cutie pie too, so I joined in. "We're freshman," I said smiling. "We don't wanna be late. Can you show us?"

"I wish I could," he responded, with a smile. "I'm late for class too. Go straight down that hall, make a right, and go all the way to the end. You'll run right into it." He smiled again, but wider, showing every white tooth in his mouth. "Hurry, you don't want detention," he said, pointing toward the way we needed to go.

We took off running with only about a minute remaining. The schedule said 101-Science, but we assumed it was a lab, because we stopped passing students after about one-third of the way down the hall. It seemed strange, but we kept running and running, without even looking at the numbers above the doors. We were almost at the very end of the hall, when the buzzer went off in my head telling me we'd been had. *What kinda jerks were we gonna have to put up with in this school*? I thought.

As soon as I put my hand on the knob to turn the door, the first period bell sounded like a piercing siren. I turned the knob anyway, verifying that it was locked. With no one in sight, Lisa and I turned to head back to civilization.

"He got us," she said, looking to see if I was as upset as she was.

For me, I didn't care that we had been tricked. I was fearful of Mr. Evan's big monstrous looking self, seeing us walking the halls. If he did, we would be getting a phone call home. My Aunt Laurie would literally want to put my head on the chopping block, and Lisa's mom wouldn't be too happy about getting a call either. As a matter of fact, Lisa's mom was a teacher at a nearby school, and had said on several occasions that she'd have no problem marching up to our school to show her who was running things. We looked at each other like we knew what the other person was thinking and sprinted down the hall.

After several minutes of searching and asking a few class-cutters where our class was located, we finally made it. Out of breath, I peeped through the small glass opening and watched the teacher pace back and forth in front of the class. The petite woman held a small clipboard and was talking to the students like they were cadets in the army.

Instantly, I pushed Lisa in front of me so she could enter first. Quickly, she darted to the side and slipped behind me, leaving me right back where I started. I huffed.

"Scaredy cat," I whispered.

Without wasting anymore time, I opened the door, only to have all eyes stare directly at me. It was like walking into a funeral with a skimpy outfit on.

I felt so out of place, I started to turn around and walk out until Ms. Ford asked, "Can I help you?"

Lisa stuttered, "I…I…I think we…we…got the wrong

room."

"Oh, yeah? Let's see your schedules." Like lightening, she approached us and snatched the schedules from our hands.

Everyone in the class was seated stiffly, facing the front like military soldiers. So I straightened my posture and stood like a soldier too. While Ms. Ford took about two minutes to compare our names with her master list, I surveyed the room. All of the chairs were lined up neatly five to a row, one behind the other. The first person in each row seemed to be watchdogs, checking out every move Lisa and I made.

"Welcome to your hardest class," Ms. Ford finally said. She gave us both a no-nonsense look and pointed to the back of the class, "You, go back there," she said to me. "And over there for you, Missy," she told Lisa, pointing to a chair near the door.

As I headed to my seat, I had to squeeze by a boy who had his legs opened wide, stretching to the middle of the aisle. He had been watching me closely the whole time I was being scrutinized by the teacher, but in a friendly sort of way. I didn't even look him in his face good to see if he was cute, because I didn't want no trouble with Ms. Ford. She looked like she could cut you with words.

As I listened to the policies and procedures for her class, I wanted to scream out loud. *I'd rather go to jail*, I thought. The rules for her classroom were non-negotiable.

"Start the warm-up as soon as you hit the door," she babbled. "And definitely, no talking unless spoken to."

"What about the bathroom?" the same boy, who had blocked my way to my seat asked. Thank God he brought some humor to the class.

"What's your name, young man?" Ms. Ford asked.

The whole class laughed. One girl, two seats in front of me, laughed so hard she had doubled over in her seat holding her stomach.

"This is not a comedy show," the teacher snapped.

"They're laughing 'cause I'm a girl."

Ms. Ford and I both had our jaws hung low. "I apologize for that," she said, trying to collect herself.

"It's cool. The name is Mika," she said calmly. "Mika Coley."

"Okay, Mika Coley," Ms. Ford huffed. "Let's start by sitting up straight. I'd appreciate it if you sit like a lady, close your legs, and take that baseball cap off in my class."

The moment, he, she, it, or whatever it was, took off the cap, my eyes were glued to the front of the room. Her braids were long like a female, corn-rowed straight back, and she even had one hoop earring in her right ear. I could not believe this was the same person I thought was a boy earlier. She remained in a slouched position, and her Timberlands pointed proudly in the air, instead of flat to the floor.

"Okay, now let's get down to business," Ms. Ford ordered. She walked to the left side of the room and pulled off the huge roll of paper that had been covering the chalkboard. "I need everyone to copy this chart down immediately. You're going to need it for tomorrow's quiz."

"Dang, Ms. Ford. Cut us a break!" Mika shouted. "You killin' us on the first day. You belong in the military, not in a school."

We all wanted to laugh, but wouldn't dare from the evil look on Ms. Ford's face. She used her finger to motion Mika to stand. "Look, you don't want to tango with me," she roared.

"I might," Mika said, like she wanted a date.

Ms. Ford stepped back, trying to analyze what was just said. She began pointing her finger up at Mika, who stood 5'7. Ms. Ford was slightly shorter, but stood up to her like a giant.

"Now, I don't know what kind of sick activities you're into, but in here, I'm Ms. Ford, your teacher! And you, you're a little girl! You got it!"

"Oh, I got it," Mika said, with a slight grin.

Now, I didn't really dig Mika dressing and behaving like a boy, but there was something I did like about her spirit. She wasn't stuck-up, didn't look to be a wanna-be, and definitely didn't seem to take life too seriously. Besides, I'd pay her a twenty spot if I had it, just to keep Ms. Ford's mind off of work for a few days.

Before I knew it, the bell had rung and everyone jetted out the room before me.

"Ms. Shawna Allen," my teacher called out. "Don't be late to my class again. Next time, you might find the door locked."

"Yes, Ma'am," I replied, and hurried out the room.

As soon as I laid foot into the hall, the madness began, and Lisa was nowhere in sight. I couldn't believe she left me in the midst of chaos. Hundreds of students walked through the halls, sneaking in their few minutes of freedom and loud conversations before the next bell rung. I wasn't about to be late for my next class, so I looked down at my schedule and checked the room number.

My attention was diverted when a short, pretty young girl with jet-black curly hair strutted through a blockade of students. Among them, Mika was standing tall in the center. With her baseball cap cocked to the side, she made comments to the young girl under her breath, while the other members of the group snickered. When the girl turned back just to roll her eyes, I figured something deep was going down. I watched closely, along with others who whispered and made jokes. I had no idea what was going on and didn't really need to care. Instead, I needed to get to my class.

As the girl held her head high, she walked right past me. I thought about asking her for help since she was alone, just like me. She seemed to be normal, except for the four rainbow wristbands wrapped around her arm. I stared her down, trying to decide if I would say something to her.

I could tell from her English book that she was a sophomore, because Shanekwa carried the same book, but something told me not to bother her. The grim look on her face showed she was ready to beat somebody down to the ground, so I turned to find someone else to ask.

As soon as my body turned to walk off, I bumped directly into Shanekwa. "Girl, I was late for my last class," I whined. "Help me find my second period — gym class. After that, I'm good, 'cause I went to the other classes yesterday. This 'A' day 'B' day stuff got me trippin'."

Shanekwa smacked her lips, and I took off following her like she was my tour guide. She slowed down just a bit, as we got ready to pass Mika and her crew, who were now congregated by the lockers near the stairs.

"Be sure to stay away from them." Shanekwa pointed to their huddle.

"Yeah, I know. They're up to no good. But that Mika is funny. She definitely gets the class clown award today." I laughed, thinking about her funny personality.

"Yeah, she also gets the dyke of the year award."

I nearly choked. "Now, I can see she dresses like a boy and all, but that doesn't mean she's a dyke."

"Yes, stupid. It's official. The word is out. She was a dyke last year, and she's one this year too."

"I don't believe it. People are always spreading rumors."

"This isn't a rumor. Keep on, and you'll be a fem soon."

"What's a fem?" I asked, feeling like a complete idiot.

"A fem is a stupid girl who dresses like a girl, looks like a girl, and acts like a girl, but they like girls too."

"Ugh!!!!!" I was starting to get a headache.

"And the girl you think is so funny is considered a Dom. You know, like Don Juan, the pimp." Shanekwa had to laugh at herself on that one.

"Well, I'm glad you told me, but that Mika is still funny."

"Okay, but don't laugh at her jokes. Or, you might be laughing on her pillow soon. I hear she turns them out."

"Who?" I asked, not understanding what she was talking about.

"Her girlfriends, her fems, stupid. She targets cute girls like you, does what she wants, and throws them away when she's done. Just look for the rainbow colors. That's what they like to wear to identify themselves."

Instantly, my mind drifted back to the young girl who had walked pass me. *Nah*, I thought. She was too cute, and dressed like a real girl too.

"Maybe that's why Mika stayed back, so she could have first dibbs on the fresh meat coming into the school," Shanekwa joked. "That includes you, boo, so keep your distance."

"Well, truth be told, you do have on multi-colored socks today." I covered my mouth so Shanekwa couldn't see my full set of teeth, 'cause that comment was hilarious.

"Forget you," she snapped, and rolled her eyes.

"Man, this is too much for one day," I said, reaching my next class. "I'll catch you and Lisa at lunch."

* * *

I watched the long hand on the clock move in slow motion, waiting for the three o'clock bell to ring. My last class, history had me almost in sleep mode. Although my body was tired, it was time to perk up. Ever since lunch, I had been studying the list Shanekwa gave me, listing six boys who were potential hook-ups.

One boy in particular, Wayne, had a star by his name.

Shanekwa said he was on the football team, and had plenty of paper. I didn't want to be considered no gold digger, but I didn't want to hook up with no broke dude either. Broke guys were a no-no.

My Aunt Laurie always said that my father didn't have a pot to piss in or a window to throw it out of, that's why he never came around. He would send Christmas, Birthday, and other special event dollar store bought cards that had one word written in them. I guess no one ever told him a simple visit would do the trick. I still loved him, even though he left me to fin for myself.

Some girls I know, without their fathers in their lives, tend to build up hate in their hearts. Not me though, I've always been taught to forgive, no matter what the charge is. I laughed at myself, thinking about how Aunt Laurie and church was rubbing off on me.

Maybe one day my father will get smart enough to know that I need him and he needs me. I just hope it's before he kills himself on those drugs. He thinks I'm too naïve to know, but I surely know right from wrong, and he is dead wrong.

Ring!!! Ring!!! At the sound of the bell, I jumped up and was the first one out the door. The plan was for me to grab my stuff and meet my girls outside of the gym. Shanekwa claimed we needed to hit the bathroom before we entered the gym. She was used to getting glossed up, so I hoped she had enough supplies for me too.

The third floor stairwell was packed. We were scrunched together like sardines, trying to make it down the stairs. I checked my watch, and nearly pushed a few students down the steps, trying to get to my locker on the first floor.

For some reason, I could feel someone watching me. I turned to my left, and there he was, the guy who had sent us to the wrong classroom earlier. I started to say something evil to respond to the slick look he was giving me, but what he got next was good enough.

Out of the blue, a left hook caught him in the jaw. His eyes grew so large, they appeared to be popping out of his head. As soon as he was able to dodge his way away from the middle of the huddle, I could visibly see two girls on the second floor landing throwing punches like Mike Tyson and Lenox Lewis. Hit after hit, they went for blood.

One girl was visibly larger than the other. She had her opponent's head locked between her arms, and was banging her head repeatedly against the railing. Cheers came from everywhere. Everyone around me tried to push their way back toward the wall, realizing this was no ordinary fight.

I instantly froze when the girl getting beat like she stole something raised her head. It was the same pretty girl I had seen get joked on by Mika's crew earlier.

In my trans-like state, I heard someone yell, "Finish her, Carmen, you know what to do!"

I watched closely for a moment, realizing that Carmen was the thick broad who fought like a dude, and was being cheered on by a large group of people. I wanted to get out of the hallway fast, 'cause I wasn't sure what was about to go down. The fight was so intense it could only get worse. But strangely, something in me couldn't leave that poor girl alone.

I panicked at the sound of the next comment. "Do her now," one girl taunted, like she was about to break out a knife. I was scared to death. I wasn't used to going to school worrying about getting stabbed.

"Ahhhhh…Miasha is gettin' the beat down!" a thuggish looking boy shouted. At least now I knew her name.

Amongst the cheering and ranting, a loud thunder of noise burst through the door. Mr. Evans and Mr. Whales, our Assistant Principal, came haul-tailing up the stairs. What they didn't know was that mace was gonna be needed to control this bunch. Before I knew it, Mr. Evans had grabbed Miasha by her collar and dragged her out of the crowd. When she lifted her face, I wanted to cry. Blood dripped from the cuts and bangs, and her left eye was completely shut.

"I can't believe you fighting over Mika!" he yelled.

My mouth dropped open. "Oh, snap. This is deep," I mumbled to myself. "Girls fightin' over girls. They need Jesus." I shook my head and followed the students in front of me out of the stairwell one by one.

A female teacher waited at the bottom of the staircase as instructed by our Principal. She asked each and every one of us if we had seen what happened.

One by one, I heard people say, "No, sorry, didn't see nothin'."

As soon as it was my turn, I pumped myself up with courage, ready to tell how that five foot eight giant hit Miasha first. The highlights of the fight were already rewound in my mind. I was just waiting for my turn.

"Hi, I'm Shawna," I said boldly. "I saw…" Just then, Mika's smile hit me. She leaned up against the wall with her hands in her pocket and shot me the warmest grin I had seen all day.

"Did you see anything?" the homely teacher asked.

"No," I said quickly, and jetted past.

Mika motioned for me to come over, so I headed her way. I wanted to let her know that people were commenting in the hall that the girls were fighting over her, and she should watch her back. She seemed real innocent, so I wasn't sure who to believe. All I knew was the scuffle Miasha was in, left her bruised and humiliated.

Before I could reach Mika, Shanekwa rolled up and swooped me by my shoulders, like a mother protecting her child from disaster. "I know you ain't goin' over there to talk to that dyke?" she said, in between gritting her teeth. "You wanna get your behind beat next?"

"What are you talkin' 'bout?" I asked, being naive.

"That girl, Miasha, just got beat up by Mika's new girl. Now, you next if you keep it up."

"I like boys. You know people with an Adams apple?" I said with sarcasm.

"Winch, don't play me. What were you goin' over there to talk about then?" She stood with her hands on her hips, like this was a straight interrogation.

I shrugged my shoulders, looking real dumb. "She told me to come over there for a second."

Shanekwa was pissed. She stormed away from me, and at that same moment, Lisa walked up. "What's up with her?" she asked.

"I'm clueless," I lied.

Lisa and I walked into the packed gym, only to see Shanekwa with her arms folded and lips poked out toward me. The bleachers had been pulled down, and all the activity clubs had tables set up in every corner of the gym, so Shanekwa couldn't get to where we were standing easily. I wanted to get involved in something, but was too stressed. I wanted Shanekwa to know I wasn't interested in Mika at all. She knew I was brought up in the church, so it was killing me to know why she was behaving like that.

Although Lisa was with me, I felt lonely. Sitting down, trying to re-focus, I whipped out my crumbled up list that had the names of several guys on it. I needed to meet a nice guy to take all of my drama away. I'd never had a real boyfriend before, but it had been on my things to do list for quite some time.

Back in May, when my mother last visited, she even asked, "Shawna, you can't buy a boyfriend, huh?" I ignored her, cause I figured by the time I saw her again, I'd be a senior anyway.

"The Lord must hear prayers," I mumbled softly under my breath, as a brotha with dark, silky skin walked right up on me and Lisa, with his pen in hand.

"Can I call you tonight?" he asked.

"Sure," Lisa answered.

I was devastated when I found out he wasn't talking to me. I stormed over into the corner, giving them some space, and sat back to watch everyone else enjoy the afternoon. Lisa talked to her new friend for over an hour, while I watched Mika perform.

It didn't take long for me to realize that Mika was considered top dog at Drew High. All the underclassman and seniors worshipped her like she was some kind of God, except for Shanekwa, of course. So many people, both girls and guys, walked up, giving her dap or slapping her hand like she was the bomb diggidy. I noticed that she was surrounded by either extremely attractive girls, or chicks who were supposed to be considered it. You know, the type of girls everyone wanted to be with.

Silently, I envied them. Not because they were around Mika, but because I seemed to be alone, once again. It was starting to be an unchanging factor in my life. My parents didn't seem to care too much. The boys weren't really checking for me, and now the only girls I know in high school, are doing their own thing.

"Uhh." I let out a soft sight and plunged my hands through my hair. I thought about how many guys were in the gym, and how none were even considering me. Was it because I looked like I still wore training bras? Or, was it because my gear wasn't fine enough? Whatever the fact may be, people can say what they want about Mika. I ain't gay or nothing, but she was the only one who smiled at me today.

Within minutes, everyone started exiting the gym. Once outside, I searched for the right bus among the ten buses lined up along the curb. I didn't want any mess from Aunt Laurie, so I took my five o'clock curfew serious. I didn't look for Lisa, or Shanekwa either. Maybe I needed to be solo for a minute, maybe become a little more independent.

Before long, I found my bus and made it home just before five. The rest of my evening was spent on homework and watching a little television until my aunt got home.

She talked my head off, asking me all sorts of questions about my day. I told her about my smart mouth science teacher and how boring history was. I even told her about the fight I witnessed, but I didn't tell her about the rumor with Mika and the girls involved in the fight.

"You meet any cute boys?" she asked.

"Nah." I shook my head like I didn't care.

"Good," she shot back. "Just checking to see if I need to come up there to check on things." She smiled.

"Aren't you comin' up to school in a couple of weeks?"

"For what?"

"Back to School Night." *Oops*, I thought. Maybe I shouldn't have mentioned it. I might not be academically ready for her to meet my teachers yet. I'm just learning the ropes.

"I'll be there," she said. "Now go to bed and get some rest, chile."

I kissed my aunt on the cheek, happy to know someone loved me for me. I got ready for bed faster than a roach can scatter when the lights come on.

Before I knew it, I was ready to climb into bed, until I heard Aunt Laurie yell, "Shawna, did you say your prayers!"

I fell to my knees immediately, cause Lord knows I need prayer after today. I took my time and gave thanks and praise. I prayed for my aunt, my mother, and my father. I prayed for Lisa and Shanekwa too. And just before raising to my feet, I slipped in a quick prayer for Mika.

Teenage Bluez II

*   *   *

Three weeks had gone by without anything major going on in my life. As usual none of the boys were checking me out, my mother hadn't been coming around, and my aunt was still keeping a tight leash on me. I sat in my room with my arms crossed as Shanekwa worked on her study guide. At any moment I knew Aunt Laurie would come yelling through the door. Luckily, me and Shanekwa had just gotten back from Hillside Mall, just hanging out and passing time. Thankfully, this allowed for a little bit of fun time before working on our school work.

Our lessons had been getting progressively a little tougher at school, and Shanekwa needed some extra tutoring. She knew math was my strongest subject, so I willingly helped her out once a week. It gave us a chance to talk about what was going down in school and catch up on the gossip.

Today, Shanekwa was surprisingly quiet. "Why you not saying too much?" I turned to ask her.

"Your conversation is whack," she said with sarcasm.

I held my mouth open, shocked at what she said to me. Just as I was about to let her have it, Shanekwa burst out laughing.

"I was just joking," she finally said. "No, in all seriousness. Since you want to give me limitations on what I can and can't say, I'd rather be quiet."

She glanced over her shoulder to see if I was watching her. I knew exactly what she was talking about. Even though she had mentioned stories about Mika over the last week, I made sure not to comment. I had also told her not to mention Mika's name around me, and to stop accusing me of being in her circle. I assured her that I was still into guys.

"Listen," Shanekwa pleaded with her hands on her hips. "If you're really my homegirl, you'll let me tell you this one funny story about Mika."

I smiled, thinking Shanekwa is a real slick chick, but she is my girl. Before I could even give her the go-ahead signal, she had blurted out several funny instances where Mika was involved.

I laughed at most of her stories, like when she said last year Mika went to the junior prom with a girl named Rachel. When she described what Mika looked like rolling up in the place with a black tuxedo on, I almost fainted. I couldn't believe it. Someone would literally have to show me pictures for me to believe that was true.

I thought about how Mika and I had gotten to be cool in science class, but talking about her behind her back was still funny. When Shanekwa mentioned Tongue Kissing Thursdays, I almost threw up. That was the last straw for me, and I prayed that Shanekwa had gotten the wrong information. She said that was the day when a certain group of girls left school grounds after lunch to go over somebody's house. They skipped fourth, fifth, and sixth period every Thursday like it was nothing. I was livid. My head dropped and I said a silent prayer for Mika instantly. This stuff was entertaining, but it was nasty. I felt like I needed to tell Mika what the Bible says about that kind of mess. Then I decided to just forget about it.

As the evening approached, I was still in my room holding my stomach from the laughter, when I heard Aunt Laurie's key turn in the door.

"Shawna, you ready, chile?" she yelled.

"Yes," I answered, in a long drawn out voice.

"Let me change my clothes and I'll be ready to go," she said.

"I'll be out front by the car," I answered, from my room.

Shanekwa and I walked out and slipped past my aunt's room. I headed to the front door before she could respond. I definitely didn't want her to see Shanekwa's new push up bra. That thing made her look like she had a set of double D's. Besides, a few minutes of fresh air and freedom was needed, because I knew once we got to the school for Back to School Night, I would be on lock-down.

I waved goodbye to Shanekwa and leaned against the car. As I waited for my aunt to come outside, I thought about my grades in each class. With only three full weeks into the school year, I was doing okay in most subjects, except Science and Spanish. My Spanish teacher probably wouldn't rat me out, but I knew Ms. Ford would try to ambush me. She had warned me on several occasions about paying attention in her class and to stop laughing so much at Mika.

I realized that every chance I got to talk to Mika in class, I took advantage of it. I loved feeling like I was a part of the more popular crowd, and not just a lonely nobody. Mika and I had even partnered on a group activity where you could choose anyone in class to work with. I remember when Ms. Ford made the announcement, how Mika nearly jumped across a few chairs just to get to me. I laughed, but it was cool. I loved the jokes and the attention.

"Chile, what you leaning on my car like that for?" Aunt Laurie yelled, making her way to the driver's seat.

She walked around the curb so fast, I almost didn't notice her outfit. As soon as she got in the car, I looked over to check her out. Thank goodness she wasn't gonna embarrass me tonight. There was nothing worse than a parent or guardian showing up at school with a whack outfit on, then getting ragged on the next day by everyone. I smiled at her plain black slacks and white ruffled shirt. Although her snatch-back wasn't the best hairstyle, it was better than some of the other old-fashioned styles she wore.

"Now, is there anything you wanna tell me before we get

over here in front of these teachers?"

"No," I answered nervously.

Aunt Laurie shot me a suspicious look, but never said another word until she pulled into the nearly empty parking lot. She grabbed her purse and jumped out of the car, with a notepad stuck under her left armpit.

"This does start at seven, right?" she asked.

I shook my head. I figured there wouldn't be too many parents who showed up. Over the last few days, I had asked several students if their parents were coming out, and nobody looked like they even knew what I was talking about.

One girl had even said, "Girl, Back to School Night is for nerds."

Now, I'm far from a nerd, but my aunt does care about my education. I always assumed most parents did.

When we entered the building, the first session of the night was hosted by our P.T.A president, Mr. Charles Archibald. We sat in the auditorium amongst about two hundred parents and students, and listened to him bore us half to death with the accomplishments of the school and staff from the previous year. I huffed thinking, *what does this have to do with me*?

After listening to him babble, Mr. Evans took the stage and talked about new discipline policies within the school.

My Aunt Laurie leaned over and whispered, "None of this better apply to you," she said, putting fear deep within me.

Soon it was time to transition to each of our classes. The staff made a brief announcement, instructing the parents to follow the schedule of their child at the sound of the first bell and move to the next class each time the bell rung.

"That's so cute," my aunt announced, loud enough for everyone to hear her.

"It sure is," I said, in my half-excited voice. I hated being fake.

Teenage Bluez II

At the sound of the bell, we were off to my first period class, science. Walking through the halls, I had to show my aunt where my locker was located, where we ate lunch, and anything else she asked about. I was really in a snappy mood, so most of her questions were met with short, one-word answers.

When we approached Ms. Ford's room, she was extra organized. She had a desk placed outside the door for all of the parents to sign up and grab a packet. Surprisingly, when we got in line, there were already about six parents ahead of us.

I looked around, realizing that the people who showed up were the cream of the crop. They were all students who I had pretty much expected to have their parents there. When we finally reached the front of the line, I shook my ears for clarity when I heard Ms. Ford call the woman in front of us Ms. Marshall.

Instantly, my eyes scrolled her body. I was expecting a manly looking woman since she was Mika's mother. But she was far from masculine. Her smooth skin was covered with colorful lipstick, blush and eye shadow. She was completely gorgeous.

Before I knew it, Mika appeared by her side and they entered the classroom together. My aunt signed the sheet immediately after them and followed everyone inside for the overview. We listened for nearly fifteen minutes, while Ms. Ford lectured without any interruptions.

Mika sat in her normal seat near the front, but not in her ordinary slouched position. She sat straight up like a star student. She almost had her mother fooled, until the speech was over and Ms. Ford asked to see certain parents individually.

She called Ms. Marshall over to the table, like she was personally being reprimanded. When she gave Mika a strange look and pointed to the door, I knew it was trouble. I rushed toward the door, pulling my Aunt Laurie's arm behind me. We had to get out of there before the drama began.

As I reached the door, my heart thumped when I heard my name being called. "Shawna," Ms. Ford called. "I need to speak with your mother privately for a moment."

My aunt did an immediate about face, while slightly pushing me out the door. Before I knew it, Mika and I were standing all alone in the middle of the hall.

At first we looked at each other strangely, trying to figure out what the other person was thinking. Then Mika broke the ice with her crazy laugh. For the first time, I noticed her soft side. In her long, maroon Redskin Jersey, she chewed on a straw, and made funny comments about Ms. Ford. My uneasiness was smoothed over by her ability to take the situation so lightly. We both ended up peeping through the small window, trying to figure out what Ms. Ford was talking about.

"I guess your mom is going to be pissed at you, huh?" Mika asked.

"That's not my mom. She's my aunt," I revealed. "My mom comes around once or twice a year," I said sadly.

"Umh…looks like we have something else in common besides being in trouble. 'Cause I've only seen my mother twice in my whole life."

"What?" My eyes bulged from my head. "Then who's that pretty lady in there?"

"She's my mother, but not my biological mother. I'm adopted." I really didn't know what to say until Mika helped me out. "Oh, don't feel bad for me. I'd rather be with her than my real mom. Who knows where I'd be." She grinned. "She treats me good, and I get whatever I want."

At that moment, I felt a real connection to Mika. We were both without our real mothers, and we both obviously had some hidden feelings about it all. For once, I felt like I had someone to share my real thoughts about my mother with. And I'm sure

Mika had a lot she could share too.

We stood there for nearly ten minutes, talking and having fun. Thankfully Mika was able to find some humor in the two of us standing outside the door, while Ms. Ford was clearly dogging us out inside the classroom. As they were wrapping things up, Mika and I decided to exchange numbers. She made it clear that she wasn't interested in me, but that I seemed like a cool person to talk to from time to time.

I was real pleased at how things had gone down. Who would've thought I would have the chance to hang out with one of the most popular girls in school with no bullies around, none of her hating friends, and no teachers or administrators breathing down our necks.

Mika was giving me a high five, and teaching me how to give the pound hand shake that I had seen her and her friends do on several occasions. I had just pounded my fist into Mika's when my Aunt Laurie yanked the door open.

"Oh, you got some explaining to do, young lady!" she yelled. "Get over here!" she instructed.

I slowly moved away from Mika, wondering what Ms. Ford had actually said.

"What's this I hear about you flirting in class, and with some girl at that? Are you Mika?" she asked, looking Mika dead in her face.

"Yes, I am," Mika replied.

"Well, when your mother comes out here, she and I both will explain to you that you are not to have any contact with this girl here!" She pointed so close to my face, I thought my eyeballs were getting ready to be poked out. "Do you hear me, Shawna Allen!"

Whoa, she was calling me by my full name. I knew I was in trouble, but I had to help Mika. "Aunt Laurie, she hasn't done anything to me."

"Not yet. Your teacher told me how she distracts you from doing your work. And you sitting up in class, smiling and laughing at her jokes like some fool."

"She can't make me laugh," I said, defending Mika.

"You two must think I'm stupid," my aunt blurted out. "Young lady, you are rebelling against God!" She looked Mika dead in her face. "In the Good Book it teaches us that lust is wrong, and especially within the same sex. Go home and read Leviticus 18:22. You should not lie with men as with women!"

I covered my face. "Ms. Ford thinks I'm into lesbianism?" I asked, surprised by my aunt's comments.

"No, she doesn't know for sure. But she can see you getting caught up. Honey, you are young and dumb, and will be spending the rest of the week learning about God's word on lesbianism. You already know it's wrong!" she shouted. "But I want a full report on why!"

Mika stood stiffly, still chewing on her straw. She was silent, but allowed a slight grin to seep through her lips. As my aunt yanked me away and pulled me down the hall, she waved humorously and shot me a smile.

* * *

Four weeks later, I giggled as I walked pass Mika, like I didn't even know her. Headed to my second period class, I thought about how we had secretly become good friends and did a great job hiding it. During school hours, we barely talked for fear that my aunt would find out, and come to the school to kick my butt from one end of the hall to the other. But behind closed doors, we snuck regularly to talk on the phone for hours. We talked mostly about our parents, or lack of, and about our plans after high school. Strangely, we never talked about Mika's preference in males or females. I knew from her actions that she wasn't interested in boys, but I made sure I talked about a few from time to time, to keep her from being interested in me.

I had even invited Mika to my church this week, hoping she would accept the invitation. I figured if Aunt Laurie saw her in church, then she'd have mercy on her, and let her call the house sometimes. Even though most things were going well with me and Mika, she said she would have to pass on church. I asked her how she could pass on God, but she got offended, so I left it alone.

I sat in class, thinking about how Lisa and I weren't as close as we used to be. In my heart, she was still my best friend. I just wished she knew more about unconditional friendship. It seemed as though she stopped calling me as often, and we hung together less and less at school. As soon as a few rumors started circulating about me hanging around Mika, she hung me out to dry. It hurt my feelings a little, but it taught me a lesson on true friendship.

I turned my head slightly in the midst of daydreaming, and realized Mika was playing around outside my classroom. The door was wide open, so I figured some of my classmates would eventually see her too. I tried to ignore her so nobody would get the wrong impression. Surely, I didn't want to be labeled one of Mika's girlfriends by seventh period.

Mika mouthed all kinds of words, trying to get me to understand. I was so busy rotating my stare back and forth from Mika to the teacher that I never caught what she was saying. Suddenly, Mika's finger curled as she mouthed, *come here*.

Shoot, I thought. *This girl is gonna get me in trouble.* I darted from my seat and asked my teacher for a bathroom pass. He gave me the okay and scribbled *bathroom pass* on a piece of paper with his signature.

Once outside the door, I didn't see Mika. Had she left? Why would she have me go through all of that if she was gonna leave? Or maybe she got in trouble? I headed to the bathroom anyway, just so I could validate my whereabouts if the cameras were watching.

As soon as I walked inside the bathroom, Mika was stooping down on the ground with a straw hanging halfway out her mouth.

"What's up?" she asked nonchalantly.

"I should be asking you," I responded. "You must want something important, since you're hanging around outside my class."

"I just wanted to see you."

"For what?" My expression showed that I was confused. Mika looked at me strangely. So I turned to the mirror to avoid her gaze. I played in the mirror, letting my finger twirl around with a few strands of my hair. "So, you not going back to class, huh?"

Mika ignored me. She stood and walked my way. She had a fresh set of braids, and the oil shimmered in the mirror. She stood behind me and looked into the mirror like she was my dude. I couldn't help but notice that the two of us standing there together appeared bizarre.

"Well, I gotta go back to class," I said, feeling a little uneasy.

Mika cupped my chin like she was trying to softly wipe something off my face. "What you tryna get into after class?" she asked.

"The next class," I answered, knowing that I was being smart.

"You know what I mean."

I shrugged my shoulders. "What can we do but go to class, or get caught in the hall? I definitely don't need any trouble." I smiled, even though I felt uncomfortable.

Mika had a weird look on her face. She shocked me when she moved in even closer. My initial reaction sent me backing up, smack dead into the wall. She capitalized on the moment and stuck her arm up on the wall, positioning herself like a full fledge guy. She looked like she wanted me. I mean really wanted me!

"Look, me and some of the girls are going over Carmen's house. You comin', or you scared to leave school?"

"Scared? I don't think so," I responded, with confidence.

"We go there every Thursday. You'll have fun. Trust me." She grinned.

Oh snap, I thought. She thinks I don't know she's talking about Tongue Kissing Thursdays. I played it real cool though.

"My aunt is expecting me home by 3:20. She gives me exactly twenty minutes after the bell rings, so I don't wanna test that."

"Alright then, but Lisa's coming. So, I guess she can tell you all about it."

"Lisa? Nah…I don't believe it."

"Why not? Everybody wants to be down with us. We're just going for a little bit of fun. You know, get out of here for a little while. It's harmless."

Now, I didn't normally submit to peer pressure, but for some reason, I didn't want to be left out. I knew skipping school was wrong, but being a loner was even worse. I went back to class and thought about how I would handle Mika just as the bell rung.

Immediately, I gathered my things and headed toward the south stairwell that was almost deserted, with the exception of the girls who were ready to jet from school grounds. By the time I realized what was going down, we had gone down the backstairs and crept out the side door. No one knew we were even gone. I kept looking behind me, thinking security or somebody would be trailing us. I was a nervous wreck, but the other five girls walked without expression. Mika grabbed my hand, sensing my edginess as we crossed the basketball court.

"Don't worry," she said. "We're good." She laughed like she had done this a hundred times before.

When we finally reached the path to Carmen's house, I glanced back at Lisa, who walked next to a girl who I had never even seen before. One thing was for sure, I recognized her rainbow wristband.

Inside Carmen's house, we all sat around eating chips, fritos, and drinking Walmart brand sodas. Although tense, I thought, *this isn't so bad after all*. It gave me a chance to bond with Lisa again, and hang out with the most popular girls.

When I saw Lisa get up and move to another room with two other girls, I was shocked. Mika and I were now all alone, but I wanted to know where Lisa was going. I didn't want to be a miniature preacher, but I would to save my friend.

I looked at my watch, realizing it was almost three o'clock and Aunt Laurie would be expecting me to call her soon. So I called Lisa's name to see if she was leaving with me. Before I knew it, Mika had grabbed my hand and led me to the couch. At that moment, I had to think fast on my feet. I had mixed emotions. I knew I shouldn't have been there anyway, and deserved what was about to happen. After all, I set my own self up.

Strangely, as Mika rubbed me, everything about her felt like me. Although she looked rough, her hands were soft, in a disgusting kind of way. She was gentle, but the intent wasn't right.

I knew right from wrong, and my long pause revealed that I wasn't down. Another girl's tongue in my mouth, *no, no, no, baby*, I thought. I closed my eyes to say a prayer, 'cause the devil had to be a liar.

Mika must have mistaken the closing of my lids as a sign to make her move. Her lips touched mine and I freaked out. I jumped up on top of Carmen's couch like a wild, untamed animal.

"You tried to trick me!" I yelled. "I thought you were really my friend."

"I am," Mika said calmly. She tried to keep attention off us, but the others had now come back in the room.

"What is this crazy chick doing standing on my mother's couch?" Carmen asked.

"This Tongue Kissing Thursday mess ain't for me!" I shouted and looked over at Lisa, who obviously agreed. "You got me all wrong. All I wanted to do was be your friend. I thought by not judging you, you'd eventually see the wrong in what you stand for."

Mika leaned back on the couch, with her legs wide open. She listened, but didn't seem to care. "Get this little girl outta here," she finally said. "Get home before your aunt calls, little girl!" she shouted.

At the thought of my aunt, I jetted out the house, with Lisa on my heels. I didn't care how bad Mika talked about us. We ran as fast as we could and never looked back. I wanted to punch myself in the face for even leaving school. My instincts told me what was up, but I ignored them. I also realized that in life, bad things will come your way, and bad people too, but because I'm a child of God, I was able to get away.

* * *

Six days later, Lisa and I were considered outcast. We walked the crowded halls of Drew Hill and endured the faint whispers from behind. Huddles filled with different personalities and cliques threw out their comments. Even some teachers stared us down with suspect looks.

"DejaVu," I mumbled under my breath, as I strutted like a

runway model.

I remembered the day when Miasha walked the halls and was mocked by everyone. She held her head high, and I decided that I would too. The only difference was there wouldn't be a rainbow bracelet on my wrist. I wasn't going to let people who shouldn't be looked up to, ruin my self-respect. And I wasn't about to become a high school statistic. I looked at Lisa and knew she felt the same way.

Lisa and I both realized we had strayed away from our principles and values, but at least we got back on track. Some of our friends, who'd heard the rumors, still looked at us strangely. However, that was nothing compared to the writing on the bathroom wall.

When we entered the bathroom, our mouths dropped. Written with a bright red permanent marker the words *Lisa and Shawna* were written largely across the top wall. And right below that, DYKE, FEM and CONFUSED followed. I huffed and laughed it off, even though it hurt a little bit. I knew I would have to be strong for a long time coming, especially since the writing was permanent.

In the end, I took it as a lesson learned and sucked it up. Be attracted to the opposite sex even if they aren't attracted to you. I smiled. *It would be a funny story to tell my husband in the near future*, I thought.

Teenage Bluez II

FIVE THE HARD WAY
by Kwiecia Cain

"GHETTO GIRLS," two words that have a million different meanings. Some people think girls who live in the ghetto are dirty because they don't have materialistic things. Others think girls from the ghetto are stupid and have no education because they talk improperly or depend on the government for money. Well, let me tell you my interpretation of "Ghetto Girls". Ghetto girls are normal females who seem to make different choices in life — like my mother always says, it's *all about choices*.

Take me for instance, J'Naye Wilson, if you saw me on the streets you would never think I'm from the hood because I carry myself with class. You wouldn't think my parents work hard everyday and still depend on the government for assistance to take care of me and my older brother, Alan. That's because of the way I carry myself.

My momma always told me life is about choices, make good choices and get good results. With that said, I vowed to be successful in life and I will always look the part. I was blessed with a caramel complexion, thick black hair that hangs a little pass my shoulders, a pretty smile with deep dimples that any girl would die for, and a nice petite frame that adds the icing to my cake. So looking at me you can't tell I'm from the projects.

Now don't get me wrong, I'm not living on top of the world

and I got problems of my own. But there are some chicks I would refer to as hood rats. I mean really, you can look at them and instantly know they are from the hood. As for me, I refuse to make a fool out of myself. At seventeen years old, I make sure my grades are good at school, I work a decent part-time job, and I ain't popping no babies out any time soon. My friends say I'm harsh and judgmental, but I think I just keep it real and strive to make it to the top. Too bad I can't say the same for my closest friends; they all got a piece of the bad life.

Take my girl, Sherita, she got it bad for real. Her mother got hooked on crack and walked out on her when she was about ten. The role of playing the woman of the house fell on her very early. Her dad works three jobs to try to support them, but the stress got the best of Sherita. Last year she dropped out of school. We didn't know if it was for a good reason or because of her fake aches and pain. We think she conjures up these elements for attention, but only God knows the truth. With her long stringy hair and slender shape, she is a problematic red-bone. But as her best friend, I'm there, whenever, wherever. But I stay in her ear about going back to school and getting herself together. Even I know there is more to life than looking good.

Next you have my girl, Ma'Isha, who is the type that doesn't appreciate the finer things sometimes. She's in school, but doesn't really care what her grades look like. I mean, she is getting kicked out every other week. And then there is her poor mother, all she wants is the best for Ma'Isha. But Ma'Isha doesn't listen, she's always worrying and disrespecting her every chance she gets. She just does what she wants and carries her mother like it's nothing. Strangely, she doesn't look like the disrespecting type. She's really pretty and looks innocent, but she will throw them hands up as soon as somebody looks at her wrong. She is spoiled rotten and thinks the world revolves around her. But that is my girl, and I would take on the world for her any day.

Then there is my best friend, Karen. She used to be a daddy's girl. With light skin and long hair, she has a body that every guy dreams about. One day her whole world changed when her father came home and announced he had another family and was leaving to be with them. That took a big toll on Karen, so she ended up spending all her time with Jemmelle, her drug-dealing boyfriend. When it was all said and done, she ended up making the biggest mistake of her life, *having his baby*. Ultimately, her mom threw her out, so she moved in with Jemmelle. Now she has to work two jobs during the day and attend school at night just to make ends meet, and it's really starting to bring her down.

Lastly is my girl, Mika. We are somewhat alike. She takes school serious, and is definitely going to make it on her own. What beats her down is her mother; she never spends time with her mom because she is always out selling her body to everybody and their grandfather. Letting her men ruin her life and running behind them is her focus. This is exactly why Mika has no father figure. Not to mention her family issues that always seem to slap her in the face.

Anyway, we all live in the same apartment complex and have gone to school together since pre-k. We decided back then we would be best friends to the day we died. In the six grade, we formed a clique called, **"FIVE THE HARDWAY"** and we've been inseparable ever since. We even opened up a bank account after getting our first paychecks from McDonalds, where we all still work. That account has about $1,200.00 in it right now. We plan on saving up until after graduation, then we will try to buy our own place outside these raggedy apartments we live in. I smile every time I think about our goal — *one day we'll all be able to better ourselves and do great things in life. Together, forever, Five The Hardway.*

Teenage Bluez II

* * *

50 Cent singing, *If I was your best friend I want you round all the time*, was the ring of my cell phone that woke me up out of my deep sleep.

"What?" I answered, knowing it was one of my girls.

"Girl, it's me, Karen. Wake up, I need your help." I could hear the desperation in her voice. "The police just kicked down the apartment door and arrested Jemmelle for possession. They found over three pounds of marijuana," she cried.

"You are lyin'! Where are you right now?" I said, jumping up out of bed.

"I'm next door at Bianca's house. Can you come pick me up? I don't want to stay at this girl's house. And from the looks of things, I won't be able to get my stuff until the morning, cause they searching that joint. The only reason they let me leave is because of the baby," Karen said, rather hostile.

"Come on, Karen, it's 3:45 in the morning. Can't you stay there 'til at least 6?" I whined.

"Girl, no. If you was here, wouldn't I come get you?"

She was right and I knew it. "I'm on my way. I'ma blow the horn when I'm out front. So have my baby girl wrapped up because it's cold out there. Where is all the baby stuff at anyway?"

"Oh, please believe I got Shamari's stuff up out of there. It's just my clothes."

"Just be glad they let you get her stuff out and leave," I responded.

"Yeah, I know. Come on!" she yelled, into the receiver.

"A'ight, I'm on my way."

"J'Naye, hurry!"

"Can I get a thank you?" I retorted through the phone. "Sometimes you got to remind people to have manners," I said, as I smacked my lips.

"A'ight, thanks girl. I owe you," she stated, as we hung up.

I jumped up and threw on the same jeans I had on earlier and slid my feet into some slippers. Tiptoeing pass my mother, I eased the door open and walked out. When I got outside, all I saw were junkies shooting up and the sound of people having sex behind the huge trashcans. *Man, I can't wait to get outta here, this is the worst,* I thought as I walked to the car. Not wanting to ride by myself, I decided to call Mika so she could ride with me.

"What?" Mika answered, with a grumpy voice.

"Wake up and ride wit' me to go get Karen," I said, ignoring her attitude.

"Where she at?"

"Girl, I'll explain it to you in the car. Just come on."

"A'ight, come around to my building," she said, hanging up the phone.

Mika lived all the way at the back of our apartment complex. When I pulled up in front of her building, she was standing out front looking mad.

"What's wrong wit' you?" I asked, as she got in the car.

"First off, I'm sleepy! Second, I wake up and see that Ashley has snuck her grown butt out the house again. I know she out here with some boy. I wish my aunt would come get her grown butt," she sighed and looked out the window. *Mika is going to let her family and their issues kill her,* I thought, while she continued to vent.

"Anyway, how you get Garrod's truck, and what's up with Karen?"

"Well, Garrod is on a cruise with his peoples, so he told me I could keep his truck until he came back, which won't be until next week." I looked over to see her expression. "Karen called me, talking 'bout come get her and the baby cause The Po-Po

Boys busted Jemmelle with three pounds of weed on him," I stated, answering all of Mika's questions. She didn't comment, she just shook her head. "So what's up with Ashley?" I asked, trying to drop the whole Karen conversation.

"Girl, all I know is she chills with like seven different dudes every week."

Poor Mika, now her family got her hooked up in some ole Players club mess.

"I called my aunt and told her she needs to come get her grown daughter cause I'm dealing with enough right now. Do you know she had the nerve to tell me she sent her over cause she wants me to talk to her," she smirked.

I could see the frustration on her face. Mika giggled and looked out the window again. "Okay, and have you talked to her, cause it's clear she is out of control?" I wanted to know what it was that Ashley had done to get shipped to Mika's.

"Yeah. She said after she slept with her mother's boyfriend, she couldn't accept her back, so she sent her over there for us to deal with her. Like I'm her mother," Mika stated.

"You are lyin'!" I had heard enough. Just then my phone rang. It was my honey, Garrod. "Hey, boo," I answered.

"I didn't expect you to be up this time of morning. I was gonna leave you a message."

"Yeah, I wish I was sleep, but I gotta get Karen. Jammelle got locked up again."

"Umh… Well, I just wanted to hear your voice before I went to sleep. Call me tomorrow when you get a chance."

"A'ight baby."

"I love you!" he stated. *Not the "L" word, I guess I do love him. Let me just go with the flow.*

"I love you too," I said, ready to hang up.

"Ay!" Garrod said, right before I hung up.

"What's up, babes?" I answered.

"Think about me!" he said, being sweet as usual.

"I will!" I hung up.

"Girl, stop blushing, we all know you in love! The funny thing is y'all in love and haven't been together that long," Mika said, ruining my moment.

"No, y'all don't understand. That's my baby, and time isn't everything," I said, with a funny feeling in my stomach.

My girl was right. I was blushing and I just couldn't help but think about Garrod. He was the best thing that ever happened to me. Unfortunately, we couldn't spend too much time together because his parents were always sending him off to do internships in high profile companies.

"BEEP-BEEP!!!" I blew as we reached Jemmelle and Karen's apartment building.

"Dang, it took long enough!" Karen yelled, as she got in the truck.

"Girl, you lucky I'm here! I'm tired as I don't know what," I stated.

"Well, thank you, babes. I told you I owe you," Karen said, putting her beautiful baby girl in the car.

"Well, where you going, cause I'm tryna go in the house, I got to get up at 6:30."

"Me and Shamari 'bout to camp out at Sherita's joint, cause I don't feel like dealing with my mother right now. Besides, she got enough to deal with, taking care of my foolish brother."

"Speak of the devil," I said, spotting Karen's brother. As soon as we pulled up we spotted T.J. with a gun to some crackhead's face yelling and screaming.

"T.J., get your grown butt in the house before I beat you like you mine!" Karen yelled.

"Girl, shut up and take your butt in the house. Can't you see I'm handlin' business," he replied.

"Yeah, whateva! Little boy, you can barely hold that gun.

Now get in here before I call the peoples to come get your little butt," Karen said, waving her hand in the air as we walked into the building.

"Hey, ladies," Sherita stated, as we walked in her house.

"Hey, Rita. Do me a favor? Change her while I warm the bottle," Karen said, barely making it in the door. "Oh, yeah. Naye, can you take me to Tyson's Corner Mall in the morning? I need to pick up some things. You know I couldn't get my stuff and this isn't going to work for me," Karen said, walking to the back.

"Yeah, I'll be over after I get out of class today, I don't have to work."

"I got a surprise for y'all. I'm gonna work my stuff and we'll have our money in order a little sooner then we anticipated," Ma'Isha stated. Turning to the baby she kissed her forehead and continued. "We don't know how long Karen will be able to go on like this, and we have to get our apartment like ASAP." I could tell she was in deep thought. "Is everybody down or what?"

"You know I am," Sherita said, walking back in the living room.

"If it's going to get me and my baby a roof over our heads, I am. I don't know what's going to happen with Jemmelle." Karen's eyes looked off in a daze.

"I don't know how much longer I can take it in my house. But…" she paused. "Jamika and J'Naye are the only ones who are unsure."

"Ain't no buts," Ma'Isha cut her off.

With all eyes on me, who am I to go against the grain. I cracked a shy smile. "Don't make me regret this," I stated, as I put my hand out as if we were a football team in the huddle.

We sat in Sherita's house for about another forty-five minutes, then Ma'Isha and I rolled out. When I got home, I jumped right in my bed and went smack to sleep.

* * *

"Buzzzz! Buzzzzz!" was the sound of the loud alarm clock that woke me from my quick sleep. As I dragged myself out of bed, I suddenly heard my mother.

"Naye, come move this truck so I can get out my parking spot. You got me blocked in."

"A'ight, here I come!" I yelled back. I put my pants on, and hurried to move Garrod's truck. Finding a parking space in my neighborhood was like pulling teeth. As soon as I parked and stepped out of the truck, my mother was all up in my grill.

"Why did you leave out this house at three in the morning?" she asked, looking as if I better have a good explanation.

"Karen called because Jemmelle got locked up, and I didn't wanna leave her and the baby outside," I replied.

"What! Why did he get locked up?" my mother asked. *She is so nosey.* I ignored her question.

"Mom, I gotta get ready for school. I'll call you to explain once I'm back in the truck, I said, rushing back into the house.

Soon as I got back inside, I jumped in the shower. Then I pulled out my favorite Armani Exchange Jeans, my burgundy wet seal screen tee, an olive green blazer, and my burgundy winter chucks. To accessorize, something I always do, I threw on a couple of buttons from *Hot Topic*, and the diamond studs my daddy bought me for my birthday last month. Lastly, my cheap lil' beauty supply store shades that made me look so high-class added the final touch. *Umm, I need one of those stolen credit cards to get me some Christian Dior shades today,* I thought. Reaching under my bed, I retrieved the sensor remover, compliments of my two-day career at Old Navy. I grabbed my cell phone and car keys and rolled out.

Ma'Isha was already outside waiting for me when I stepped out the door. I knew she had a scheme planned by the way she looked at me.

"Look," I said, "our plan is for *Five the Hardway* to make it out the ghetto, and the route you're taking means you're going to be left behind."

"Girl, I'll make it, I got six more months before I get that Cosmo License and I'm going to make it. Not to mention what I'm 'bout to do that's going to put us on."

There she goes again, what is she talking about? I knew not to ask, Ma'Isha is the type to tell once she has all the facts.

"Yeah, a'ight! We'll see. It sounds illegal," I said, turning the volume up as far as it could go. We sang and danced to our go-go music all the way to Forest Hill High School.

* * *

"Dang, that TCB go-go CD makes me want to go out to the *Black Hole* or some where," Ma'Isha, stated, as we got out the truck and entered the school. When we walked into the school, it was like a runway, all eyes on us, and everybody complimented our outfits. Everybody knows our clique is known for the outfits we put together. That's what we love to do — shop and look good.

This one girl had the nerve to ask where I got my stuff from. I told her, "My closet!" I didn't like telling anybody where I get my clothes from.

Instantly, my phone rang, *If I was your best friend I want you round all the time.* As the music played, I knew it was Sherita calling to make sure nothing happened. We talked briefly and I told her I'd call her later.

As I was closing my phone, I glanced at the clock on the front of it. It was 7:30, and the late bell rang at 8:00, so that meant I only had thirty minutes in the hallway. I hurried up and threw on my MAC Lip gloss, grabbed my books, and walked around by the cafeteria area. When I got there, I saw Mika and Ma'Isha posted up on the wall talking to their dudes. So I began walking toward them.

"J'Naye!" The voice threw me off my focus of walking over to where my girls were. It was my brother, Alan. A lot of people don't believe we are related because we look nothing alike. I mean really, I'm way darker than him, and he is real light. He has red hair and freckles, and I have black hair. Anyway, I wondered why he was at my school.

"Alan, what are you doing up here?" I asked, in shock.

"I had to come get a recommendation from one of my old teachers," he replied.

"Oh! What time are you leaving here?" I asked.

"Soon. I gotta get back to my school. Why? What's up?"

"Nothin', I just wanted to spend a little time with you."

"A'ight, call me when you get out," he stated.

"A'ight!"

My brother and I used to be really close, until he went to Howard on a football scholarship and started living on campus. After talking to my brother, I noticed that it was 7:55, which left me no time to talk to my friends, so I headed off to class. When I got to class, I noticed Mariah and her crew know as, *High Passion Hunnies,* starring me down.

"Take a picture it'll last longer," I sassed as I walked pass, mugging all six of the dirty broads. Mariah wanted so badly to be like us, or be a part of our crew, but she just couldn't, she was never on our level.

"The High Passion Hunnies" are poor examples for teenagers. Don't get me wrong, yes, members of *Five the Hardway* have made mistakes, but nothing like theirs. We would never share boyfriends, let a male come between us, or

anything in that manner. As for them, it was a totally different ball game. *Shake the haters off,* I thought, as I spun around on my heels and threw my hips in their direction.

* * *

On the way to Sherita's house, I called Garrod. I just knew we were in love and would be together forever. I rapped to him for about five minutes, because I knew he didn't have much more time than that. I had to keep him on my team so that I could get his ride when needed. When I hung up, I immediately turned on my Keysha Coles CD and listened to her keep it real all the way to Sherita's house.

When I arrived at her house, I spotted T.J. standing on the front porch rapping to somebody on the cordless house phone about some money. *This little boy ain't gonna live long,* I thought.

"Hey, T.J.," I spoke, as I kept it moving into the building.

"What's up with you, Naye?" he sassed back, staring at my butt as I walked up the stairs.

"No respect!" I stated, shooting him a dirty look. He just laughed as I made it to the top of the stairs.

"Who is it?" Sherita yelled, as I banged on her door.

"The police! I have a few questions concerning a Tyrell Jones," I joked.

"Whatever." Sherita opened the door. "You know you can't change your voice."

"Where's Karen?"

"She's in the back putting the baby's clothes on. What y'all 'bout to do?" she asked.

"Probably go see my brother on campus for a hot second, and then we're going to hit the mall. Why?" I looked in her direction.

"Cause I just wanted to know!"

"Why you always clocking me, worry about yourself," I playfully retorted, as I watched Sherita pin her long Spanish looking hair up.

After several minutes of rushing Karen out the door, we dropped Sherita off and decided to drive straight to my brother's dorm room.

"Who is it?" my brother said, as I banged on his dorm room door.

"It's me, J'Naye."

"Oh, hey sis." He opened the door with a slight smile.

"What's up?" I retorted out of breath, after walking up about four flights of stairs.

"So what's good with you, sis? How's everything with school and Garrod?" my brother asked, as I took my coat off. Karen was in the truck rapping on her cell phone.

"Well, school's coming along perfect, and as for Garrod, we're doing okay. He's on vacation," I answered.

"Ummm! So, what are you up to today, you don't have to work?"

"Me and Karen are going to Tyson's Corner Mall."

"You stay at the malls. What kind of money is Mickey D's paying these days?"

I ignored his statement and watched as he focused on the mirror in front of me. Being conceited as usual, he turned from side to side, looking at his profile.

"Dang, I'm just too beautiful, ain't I?" he asked, watching me through the mirror.

"Boy, go sit down somewhere!" I said, with a giggle.

"Girl, you just don't know! Hunnies be lovin' this light skin brother here. I neva in a million years thought I would have this many females when I got to college, and I'm loving it to the fullest." He was wearing a huge smile. "I'm tellin' you, Naye, wait 'til next year when you're in college. This is the life." He locked his fingers and placed them on the back of his head.

"So, what you doing tonight?" I asked, quickly changing the subject.

"Well, I'll probably hit up this Frat Party tonight, why?"

"Just asking a question. Hey, where's your roommate at?" I asked.

"I don't know. He said he'd be right back, but I haven't heard from him. I'ma go hop in the shower and get fresh. If you get hungry or thirsty, then go 'head and grab something to eat out the fridge."

The moment he walked out the dorm room, my cell rang. "Yes, Rita," I sang into the phone. I covered my mouth and listened to what she had to say, because the sight before me had me in shock. I lowered the phone a bit and watched the scenery.

My brother's roommate walked in with a just a towel wrapped around his waist, showing off his triceps, biceps and his 8-pack abdominal chest. I stood there with my mouth wide open. I couldn't quite pull myself back together.

"J'Naye, J'Naye! Are you there?" the voice on the phone said, bringing me back to reality. I finally got my tongue to work. "What's wrong with you?" Sherita snapped. Instead of acknowledging her, I hung the phone up and turned it off, cause I knew she'd be calling back.

"Hi! I'm Ron-Ron, Alan's roommate. I take it you're his sister, J'Naye, right?" He extended his hand, trying to introduce himself.

"Yeah, how did you know?" I asked, trying to recover.

"Well, because he has pictures of you everywhere, not to mention he talks about you a lot. I'm sorry for startling you like that, he didn't tell me you were here, or that you were even coming. But it was a pleasure meeting you," he stated, kissing my hand.

"Oh, the pleasure is all mine!" I replied back.

Ron-Ron walked over to his dresser, grabbed some clothes, and walked back out the door. As soon as the door shut, I immediately turned my phone back on. I had five voicemails within those seven minutes. My brother walked in, catching me with a wide grin.

"I just met your roomie. He's nice..." He cut me off mid-sentence.

"Don't even think about it," he spat.

"I just said he's nice." I smiled and picked up my keys. "Any who, I have to go, Karen's waiting in the truck. Plus, Rita must need me by the way she's blowing up my phone."

"Be safe." He gave me a hug and I left the room dialing the phone.

"What's good, Naye?" Mika answered.

"Girl, what are you doing?" I asked her.

"Just getting out of school, waiting for Shane to pull around the front of the school. Why, what's good and why you sound like that?"

"'Cause girl, I was sitting in Alan's dorm room waiting on him to get out the shower when his roommate walks in with just his towel on. And girl, his body is to die for!"

"Girl, you lying! Where he at now?"

"He left back out, but he's a bun. He's so cute."

"Umm! Let me find out you 'bout to cheat or pull a fast one on Garrod."

"Oh, naw! I just had to tell you that. But I think he's into me cause he was looking at me with that look," I stated.

"Girl, you betta keep him on your warm-up bench, cause you never know when Garrod is gonna mess up," she swiftly replied.

"Oh, please believe me when I say, I got that covered," I told her.

By the time we wrapped up our conversation, Sherita was ringing my phone once again. I huffed thinking about having to talk to her all the way to the mall.

* * *

When I got home from the mall, there was no one home as usual. I began putting my stuff away so my nosey mom wouldn't come in asking questions. As I put away the jeans and accessories Sherita got me from my favorite store, *Delia's,* I started to check my voicemail. The first seven messages were from Garrod. Then there were four from my mommy, bombing me out because I didn't call her all day.

The last one was from Karen, "Naye, I was calling to see if you were home. I probably won't be home until tomorrow morning, 'cause my new friend doesn't feel like coming back out tonight. I don't want to ask you for another ride, but nobody is picking up their cell phones, so I'm out. Call me, bye!"

Wow, she's chilling already. Who does Karen think she's fooling? I sat in the chair daydreaming about how off the hook Karen is and how cruel she is treating Jemmelle right now. I wanted her to settle down a bit. I wanted her to start making better choices in life. *Maybe, I'll invite her to lunch and have a heart to heart talk with her*. The phone rang, catching me off guard. I answered on the first ring.

"Oh, you in the house now. Where have you been all day? And why haven't you learned to pick that phone up?" the voice said, as soon as I answered.

"Hi to you too, Mommy. I was at Alan's school, and I'm sorry, but I didn't know you called. How you know this was me, I could've been Daddy for all you knew."

"Well, you couldn't have been your father cause he's sitting next to me driving, and I just got off the phone with Alan, so you're the only one who could be in the house."

"Alan didn't tell you I was at school with him today?" I asked.

"Yeah, but that has nothing to do with you calling."

"Where y'all at?" I asked.

"Why, J'Naye?"

"Are you guys coming back tonight? And can Mika spend the night?" I said, without taking a breath.

"I don't care if she stays."

Feeling relieved, I asked her again if they were coming home, and she said yes, but it would probably be real late. After hanging up, I called Mika and told her to come over. Within the next five minutes, Mika was at my door.

"Hey, boo!" I stated, as I welcomed her into my home.

"What's up, girl? Let me see the stuff."

"What stuff?"

"Don't think I don't know. I heard all about it. You can't keep it a secret, and y'all can't keep stealing. If you get caught, we'll never make it out the hood."

"You're right," I said sadly, "But it's so easy. Karen and Rita have been gettin' these stolen credit cards for real cheap. That's how come we go to the mall every other day."

"I just don't want nobody to get in trouble." Mika paused and started to look through my new wardrobe. "I mean, you know I love to look the part too, but…"

"I know, Mika." I sat on the bed next to Mika and handed her a small Tiffany's box. She carefully took the white ribbon off the aqua box and smiled as she read the inscription on the charm dangling from the bracelet: *J'Naye, Jamika, Karen, Ma'Isha & Sherita - Five the Hardway.* She smiled and gave me a hug.

"Dang, you stole this too?"

"No, I bought it. I do work, you know. Don't worry, before

you know it we'll have our place, be finished high school and attending college," I assured her. "I'm going to get in the shower. Make yourself at home," I said, wanting to change the subject.

"Girl, shut up, acting like I ain't never been here before. I've been over here like a million times," she shot back.

I grabbed my radio and headed toward the shower, blasting my new *Mariah Carey* CD. I pretended like her comments about stealing didn't bother me, but they did. I knew I was wrong, but I had an addiction to clothes. An addiction that would have me locked up soon, if I didn't stop.

*   *   *

A week passed since Garrod had been home. He let me keep the truck because he didn't want me getting off from work and catching the Metro at night. *I guess you can do that when you're rich and spoiled with a car and a truck.* Besides, he hated coming from Potomac to pick me up, only to drive five minutes down the street.

He didn't know that I hadn't been working much lately, anyway. With Sherita's new scheme, we've been hitting all the malls within a fifty-mile radius. Ma'Isha's aunt works at MVA, and has been hooking us up with ID's and information to open bank accounts. I never knew stealing could be so easy. No matter how much we tried to get Mika in on our newfound fortune, she liked her same five-finger discount. She claims that everything else is too risky.

The ring of my cell phone was the alarm that snapped me from my thoughts.

"What's up, Karen?" I answered.

"Don't you have a half day today?" Karen asked.

"Yeah. Why? What's up?"

"Can you please do me a big favor?"

"What?"

"Watch Shamari, cause I gotta meet my friend and I gotta go to school."

"What time?"

"12:45," she replied.

I didn't believe her, but I said, "A'ight, I'll be there about 11:30 or 12:00. Karen, don't forget you gotta go and get your ID so you can open this account."

"I know, Naye. I'm gonna get him to take me first thing in the morning."

"Don't play because Aunt Peaches has been waiting for you," I snapped at her.

"Look, I gotta go. This new guy I met is beeping in on the other line."

"Who?" I asked, letting her know I had a problem with what I was hearing.

"I met this sexy dude on my way home. He was too fine, so I gave him my digits and he told me he would hit me up later."

"Wait! What about Jemmelle?" I asked curiously.

"Oh, girl, please. He's locked up and 'bout to get shipped to Ohio. I don't have time to be waiting on him. I mean really, what can he possibly do for me behind bars?"

That blows my mind about Karen; she thinks she needs a man to survive in this world, and for some reason, I just can't get with that. "Ummm! So when Jemmelle is down and out, you're not going to wait for him?" I questioned.

"No! I'm too young to be concerned about him. He should've thought about what he was doing, so I got to move on. I love him and all that good stuff, but I gotta do me, and if there's a future for us, we'll take it from there!"

I hated getting ugly with my friend, but she had to hear the truth. "Oh, so you can lay up and have a baby with Jemmelle, then when he gets locked up, you're not there for him. That's terrible, and you know what you're doing is wrong," I fussed, trying to make Karen see the truth.

"Look, J'Naye, I don't have time to sit on the phone and listen to you give me the third degree," she snapped.

"Ay, Karen, chill out with all that. I'm not trying to give you the third degree. I was just letting you know that what you're doing ain't right. Seriously, before you and Jemmelle had this baby, y'all was tight. He had a good head on his shoulders and a full scholarship to any school. Keep in mind that you got pregnant, so he was trying to take care of his responsibility." I paused to let that sink in before continuing. "Think about it, I know what he was doing is wrong, but he's always been there for you."

"I hear you, but J'Naye, you know I gotta do things my way."

"Suit yourself. But when this stuff blows up in your face, I'ma tell you I told you so."

"Oh yeah?"

"That's right."

"A'ight! But I still love ya! I'll see you in a bit."

I hung up the phone, wondering who she thought she was fooling. I knew exactly what Karen was up to, but I figured I would wait for her to tell me. She doesn't work anymore, and she hasn't been putting in any work in the malls. We have been handling things and she is on some ole' find me a good nigga mission. *Oh well, it will be good to see the baby. Especially since I have been so busy lately.*

The knock at the door startled me. It was Mika and Ma'Isha standing outside like there was a problem.

"What's wrong?" I asked.

"What's right?" Mika responded. "What's this I hear about Karen not doing her part?"

I couldn't lie. For weeks, we had been on our grind and Karen hadn't stolen a thing. But she definitely reaped the benefits.

"Yeah," Ma'Isha interrupted. "She need to get on it," she said, with a concerned look on her face.

"Ma'Isha, you need to talk to her, because Aunt Peaches is pissed that she hasn't handled her business."

Ma'Isha looked at Mika and said, "I haven't seen you steal one thing or swipe one card yet either."

Mika didn't say anything, she just shook her head. "Y'all right. I'll check Karen because I'm 'bout sick of picking up stuff for her dates. Besides, the money we're saving is for all of us to move. So, we all need to work for the money, even lover girl."

I dropped the subject and let it go. There was no reason to even talk about Karen anymore, because she was going to do things her way.

* * *

Just like that, it had been decided in a matter of minutes that we would all hang out for a *Five the Hardway* outing the weekend. We sat around chit-chatting like we didn't have a worry in the world, contemplating on where to go.

"A'ight then, I'm going, but I don't have anything to wear," Sherita said.

"Nothing to wear, Rita, shut up!" I said. "I have to be at work at 12:30. I'll barely have enough time to take a shower and find something to wear," I responded.

"Karen, you got money?" I asked.

"I got $200.00 to spend this weekend, being as though I didn't have to buy Shamari nothing because the *WIC* check came in. I got it out our mailbox yesterday and I already deposited $300.00 into our account," Karen stated.

"So you are hitting your new dude's pockets?" I snapped proudly.

Karen ignored my remark. "I noticed that the balance is over five thousand." She looked around.

"Yes, we're looking for a place now," Ma'Isha stated. We all held up our bracelets and shook our arms.

"Well, we deserve to celebrate," she spat.

"But where's the baby going while we celebrate?" Sherita asked Karen. Everyone looked at her for an answer.

"Jemmelle's mother is keeping her this weekend so I can do me," she replied.

"A'ight, so it's official, *Five the Hardway* is partying tonight, right?" Ma'Isha asked.

"Yup, I guess so! But let's go to the mall because I don't have nothing cute to wear," Sherita stated.

"Are we buying or boosting?" Ma'Isha asked? "Shoot! I want to wear something like this." She pointed to the outfit Paris Hilton was wearing in US Magazine.

"Yeah, that's real cute. I might wear something similar to that as well," Sherita stated.

Truth is I needed a trip to the mall, because I wanted to look real cute.

* * *

When we got in the truck, Karen began telling everybody about the boy she met and how she just knew they would be together. I tried to ignore her and focus on the directions to the St. Charles Mall. Then I couldn't take much more of her foolish conversation.

"What did he think about you having a baby?" I interrupted.

"Well, he got a son too, so we're on the same boat," she

responded sarcastically.

"Where's his baby mama at?" Ma'Isha asked.

"She lives in North Carolina."

I huffed, pulling into the lot as fast as I could. I didn't want to hear anything else she had to say. We entered the mall and went to work.

"Ay y'all, I got a *Hot Topic* Gift Card, so we 'bout to rack up on some pins, you hear me," Ma'Isha stated.

"Girl, why spend your gift card on that when you can buy something else, like a shirt or some shoes and just take the pins like we do?" Sherita asked, encouraging Ma'Isha to steal.

"Yeah, you right. Let me go look in the back," she said.

"Yeah, I hear you!" Mika replied.

"Oohhh! American Eagle Outfitters, come on y'all let's go in there!" Sherita shouted.

"A'ight, but I'ma need you to calm down, like seriously," I commented, as we walked toward American Eagle Outfitters.

I noticed all the new merchandise. I racked up on a lot of little Graphic T-shirts, not only for me, but for Garrod too. I bought two, and stuffed the other six in my book bag. When I reached *Hot Topic,* I noticed they had some tight jewelry. They also had the cutest Vans. I bought me two pair and some black pants, and stole about twelve different accessories. I hadn't mastered how to take shoes and stuff yet, so I pulled out my brand new check card, compliments of Aunt Peaches.

We decided to go and put all our stuff in the truck, so we could go back in with empty bags. As we reached the lower level, I became happier than a kid in a candy store when I noticed they had my favorite stores, Aeropostale and Forever 21 in there. I went in both stores and racked up on almost everything. We shopped for about two hours before sitting down to eat at Ruby Tuesdays. After splitting the bill five ways, we made our way to the truck.

Teenage Bluez II

As we were walking, we noticed there were only four of us. We turned around to see that the police officers had Mika in cuffs taking her to the holding facility in the mall. So we followed behind them, and they explained how they had caught her taking shoes from footlocker, but they had to release her because her face was never shown on the camera and she didn't have the shoes with her. After really acting ghetto and cursing the flashlight cops out we bounced. In all actuality, it scared us and we all made a vow not to steal no more. If we didn't have our own money, we wouldn't get it.

Several hours later, I headed to Sherita's house around 7:30, and everyone was ready. I began to check out everyone's outfit. It was looking pretty good.

Mika had on a schoolgirl looking outfit; a white collar shirt with the collar popped, a red tie, and a pleated skirt that was dark green, navy, yellow and red. To add to it, she rocked black suspenders worn over her shoulders, white knee-highs with a black bow right at the knee, and black pumps. She also had on red lipstick and mascara that brought out her features pretty well. She had on oval shaped white personality glasses, and her braids were in two ponytails with two big bows on each one. She accessorized with big silver hoops that read *Mika*, and a couple of cheap silver bracelets.

Sherita had on a pair of gray, dark green and black pleated Bermuda shorts, along with a black collar shirt, and a short v-neck green sweater. She also had on thick gray socks and black pumps. To accessorize, she had on big silver beads, mascara and black skull studs. Her hair was in a tight bun on the upper left side of her head.

As for Karen, she had on baggy jeans that hung low, and a black shirt that had small red polka dots all over it. She rocked red snakeskin cowboy boots that pointed from underneath her jeans. Her hair was also freshly streaked. It was bone straight with a little bit pulled up with a white bow around it on the front left side. She accessorized with vintage red earrings, which I'm guessing she got from our favorite thrift store. She wore black beads and red glasses, which she had taken the lens out, and were now just frames, but cute.

After about ten minutes of being in the house, Ma'Isha walked in. She had changed her outfit completely. She had on a purple, red and green short sleeve vest, with a white collar shirt under it, a jean skirt and vintage purple pumps she had also scored from the thrift store. She accessorized with gold and purple necklaces, which were in layers, and big lion earrings that I had fallen completely in love with. Her hair was still in a braided Mohawk as usual.

"Come on, everybody's ready, so let's rock!" I stated.

Once we got in the truck, we turned on TCB to get us hyped and rolled out. We reached the *Greendale Center* at about 8:35 p.m. The line wasn't too long, but not short either.

When we got to the door, we paid $10.00 each, got checked, and was ready to party. The first go-go band that played was some weak band that nobody knew. Everybody was in there; some crews called the Flii Boyz and 1200 were deep as a mug. As we began to party, I spotted some girl mugging us from a mile away, but I didn't say anything, I just mugged back and kept partying. As MOB started cranking, we took our picture. There were a couple dudes who used to go to elementary school with us in there, and they jumped in our picture. But we didn't mind though.

After MOB played, TCB start cranking real hard so, of course, we were dancing extra hard. We went to the front and these girls kept mugging, so we was mugging back. Then one of them pushed Ma'Isha and, of course, she got to wrecking and we jumped in it. We were punishing these girls like it was nothing. It was six of them and we still had the best of them. As the bouncers were putting us out, I saw blood all over Ma'Isha. I thought some girl got all up in her stuff, but then I noticed she had stabbed somebody.

"Yeah! We punished them hoes like it was nothing. I stabbed the mess out that big girl," Ma'Isha bragged.

"Why? You might get a charge now. What's wrong with you?" I preached.

"Girl, they don't know it was me!" she replied.

"All they gotta do is review the tapes," Mika stated.

"They don't have no tape in there! And where's Karen?" I asked, just now noticing that she was missing.

"I don't know. Matter fact, I didn't even see her fighting!" Ma'Isha stated.

"You are lying!"

"No, dead serious. She wasn't even up front with us. Call her phone!" Ma'Isha insisted.

I pulled my phone out and called her, scared to death.

"Hello!"

"Karen, where are you?" I asked.

"Girl, I'm chilling with this dude named Aaron, who went to elementary school with us."

"You where? Don't play with me! Why would you leave the club with a nigga you ain't seen since elementary school?" I asked.

"Cause he looks good girl, and he got money!" she responded.

"You trifling as I don't know what, and you better hope he bring your gold-digging tail home. And I hope you got somewhere to stay because Sherita said you can't stay with her no more." I hung up in her ear.

"What happened? I know she's not still in there?" Ma'Isha asked.

"No! This freak left with somebody she doesn't even

know!" I replied, already mad about the fight.

"You lying! She can't be that dumb. J'Naye stop playing, cause I'm already mad," Jamika said with her fist balled up, ready to do more damage.

"Girl, I'm not playing. She left!"

"Oh yeah!" Sherita responded. "She definitely can't stay at my house no more. She better go live with her mother or something."

We talked about Karen's situation for about five more minutes, then the police pulled up and began walking toward us. Ma'Isha took off running, so without question, the cops immediately chased her. Mika, Sherita and I got in the truck and pulled off too. As we were riding down the street, I began to fuss about everything that was going on.

When we got back around the way, I stopped at the gas station where I spotted Mariah and her clique chilling with some lame looking boys. I began to walk to the teller window thinking, *I wish this girl would say something cause I will beat her right here in front of everybody.* I must have had a Genie in a Bottle, because she began talking trash.

"Look what the dirty ol' alley cat drug in," she joked, as I paid for my gas.

"Mariah, one question. Where do guys looking for freaks hang out?"

"What?"

"You know the answer," I smirked. "They hang 'round dirty ol' gas stations at three in the morning. You dummy!"

She began walking toward me. Before I knew it, her hand was near my face. I glanced over at the truck, then I looked right back in her face. *Smack* was the sound that my fist made when I hit Mariah in her mouth. She immediately dropped and I stood there, talking more trash.

"I'm tired of your mouth! Always got something to say.

How does it feel to be laying on the ground?" Then I turned to look at her crew. They all just stood there. I could hear one girl saying she should have shut up.

I didn't have time to think about anything else but Ma'Isha at the moment. I was so worried. Every time I heard a siren, I drove toward the sound, hoping we'd find her.

"Girl, my hand hurt like I don't know what," Sherita said, as we pulled into the complex. We figured that Ma'Isha may have been able to catch a ride home.

"It was probably that girl's hard jaw!" Mika replied, as we all began to laugh. We all decided to camp out at my house to wait to hear from Ma'Isha.

We talked about everything we had been through over the course of the day, from the mall to the club. We even shed a few tears together, thinking about everything that was going on. I called Ma'Isha's phone, but she didn't answer. I stayed up worrying like a frantic parent until I finally dosed off to sleep.

* * *

The sound of my house phone woke me up at about 7:45 in the morning.

"Hello!" I answered.

"This is a *JCF* collect call from Ma'Isha. The cost for this call is $2.80 for the first five minutes, and .57 cents for each additional minute. If you'd like to accept this call dial five, if you don't accept the charges hang up. Please make your selection now."

After the little lady was finish talking, I pressed 5. "Ma'Isha, go 'head and break it down to me," I stated, after I was finally able to talk to her.

"First of all, let's talk about when I ran from them sorry excuses for policeman. I ran all the up Eastern Avenue and down towards Kenilworth. When I got down that way I thought I had lost them, but they was still behind me. I stopped by Moe-Moe's house cause you know he lives around there. I got something to drink and washed that blood off my hands. I changed my shirt and took that knife off my belt and cut through my jeans and cut my leg, then I cut my arm and a little of my neck. When I got a napkin and sat down to tell Moe-Moe what happened, these crackers starts knockin' on the door. But before Moe-Moe could ask them if they had a warrant, they came barging in. So they got me girl. When they brought me down here to the dirty Juvey Jail for questioning, I just sat there as they asked me all these questions about the fight."

"You didn't tell them nothin?"

"All I said was it was a group fight, cause they tried to jump me, and next thing I know, I had blood from my cuts everywhere. So they took me to some little nurse and she let them know the type of wounds I had and how deep they were. Then they said I had to stay here cause I ran from the authorities. I gotta stay here until they post my bond, which won't be until next week being as though it's Friday. Naye, call Aunt Peaches, because I forgot the Best Buy cards were in my purse."

"Dang, girl! You're such an outlaw. You not scared to talk on this phone."

"No, cause one of the girls told me she did something to this phone so it's not tapped anymore."

"So how does it feel to be in jail?" I asked.

"Let me tell you this, it's not where it's at. I only been in here for about three and a half hours, and I hate it already."

"Ummm! Bet you learned your lesson, huh?" I asked. "If you haven't, I have."

"Whateva, J'Naye! Thanks for looking out," she said, slamming the phone down.

"Who was that?" Mika asked, as she got up.

"That was Ma"Isha. I guess she's mad because she got caught."

I told them what happened and we all got quiet. We knew if she told about our credit card scam, we would all end up in trouble. Our loyalty to one another was starting to dwindle before anything could even happen. I walked away, headed to my room for a nap. Sleep was all I wanted to do. I didn't care if my girls left or stayed. I was starting to realize that we weren't really doing anything positive with our lives.

When I got up, I noticed that my mother wasn't home. I got in the shower, put on some clothes and called my mother. I didn't bother telling her what happened, cause I didn't feel like hearing her mouth. But I did tell her about Mariah and she just laughed, cause she understood where I was coming from with that girl. I also told her how Karen left with some boy and she started saying how Karen was gonna end up just like my aunt. I talked to her for about thirty minutes before she told me that she was going Christmas shopping, being as though it was right around the corner. I informed her that I wanted to go, because it was a planned outing for us. She said she would be coming to get me at about 2:30. I sat around and talk to my girls for about another hour, then they packed up and went home.

About ten minutes after they left, I sat around and thought about how much our friendship had changed since we were young. Then my phone rung, it was Karen.

"J'Naye, can you come get me? This nigga left me at the hotel and I don't have no way home," Karen said, as soon as I picked up the phone.

"No, I'm not coming to get you. Since you want to be grown and leave with that nigga, be grown and find a way home," I stated, as I hung up in her ear.

I knew we were not going to be talking anymore, so I called

Jemmelle's mother and drove over there to spend time with Shamari. Come to find out this nigga only got six months behind bars. When I left, it was about 12:45, so I rode around and talked to Garrod. Then I went in the house and lounged around until my mother came home.

* * *

After a long evening, I woke up and checked my messages the next morning. I had a message from Mika, saying I didn't have to pick her up from school, and another message from Garrod, saying we needed to talk. Since I didn't have to get Mika, I put my clothes on and was on my way out. I stopped pass my mother's and father's room and asked my father if I could have some money. He gave me $10.00 and I rolled out.

When I got to school, I spotted Jamika but we didn't say anything to each other because I guess we all felt the same way. We just needed a break and that was that. I went to class and went straight to work after school. To my surprise, none of us were working together for the next four weeks. I spotted Ma'Isha's name on the schedule, but hearing about her situation, I knew she wouldn't be in.

While studying the Schedule, I noticed Mariah buying some food. I ignored her.

I had to meet Garrod with his truck as soon as I got off. I clocked out about two minutes early and rolled out. After meeting Garrod with his truck, I went and chilled at his house.

"So, what's been going on lately?" he asked, as we sat down in his room.

I decided against telling him about my crew. I wasn't really feeling him that much anymore. I mean, I liked driving his truck, but that was it.

"Nothing much," I replied.

"You seem kinda down, Naye. What's going on?" he asked.

I couldn't hold it any longer, I had to hear myself say it. "Me and my friends, well, we've kinda fallen apart. I mean, Ma'Isha got locked up, and Karen left the club the other night with some boy, so we got to beefing. As for the rest of us, we just needed a break," I stated, looking down feeling like I wanted to cry.

"It will be a'ight. Y'all will pick back up, it's not going to be long. I mean look at how long y'all been cool," he stated, being a good boyfriend as usual.

"Maybe you're right." We talked and kicked it for about two hours, then I went home. For the first time, I realized that we are definitely in two different worlds.

Five Years Later....

Ma'Isha learned her lesson after serving two years in a Juvenile Detention Center. Thankfully, for the rest of *Five the Hardway* members, she never told on us about the stolen credit cards. She did, however, spill the beans on the entire credit card operation, excluding our involvement, of course. Inside the system, she worked hard to obtain her GED and changed her ways completely. She finally gained respect for her mother and they formed a cool relationship. She obtained her cosmetology license, and she now teaches hair at Forest Heights High School and has a nice apartment in Suitland, Maryland.

Sherita eventually enrolled in night school and graduated at the top of her class. She is a nurse at a doctor's office in Forrestville, Maryland, and plans to enroll in college to become a surgeon. She is still single and has no children. As for her brother, he is serving life and her father remarried.

After obtaining a STD from some dude she slept with,

Karen learned her lesson. Now she understands that all she needs is her family. When Jemmelle was released, he forgave her. They rented a condo and just recently got married. She finally caught up with her father and they have a tight relationship again. Her mother is also in her life, she watches Shamari while Karen goes to work. She works at a dentist office in Northwest. Jemmelle attends Tech School, majoring in collision repair.

Jamika attended Clark Atlanta University, double majoring in Dance and Art. She's a RC at the dorm and braids hair at a shop not too far from the campus. She has her own apartment back in Maryland, where she let her cousin, Ashley stay. She finally gained a relationship with her mother. She helps Jamika with her school and bills. She is also planning to get married to an intellectual guy next April.

As for me, after staying home for a year while my mother finished school, I went on to attend Berkley College in California. My major, of course, Fashion Design. Garrod and I went our separate ways, but Ron-Ron and I hooked up when he enrolled in UCLA's Law program.

Even though *FIVE THE HARDWAY* didn't keep our promise as being best friends, we did get out the ghetto, and that is the important part. We still associate from time to time, and I guess if it's meant to be, we'll come back together. At least we vowed never to steal again. We have been taught some life lessons, and I hope you were able to grasp them. Don't allow your environment and/or situations dictate who or what you will become in life. But either way the story ends, we will always remain *FIVE THE HARDWAY*, and that's what's important.

WORDS FROM
<u>THE AUTHORS</u>

Teenagers, we hope the stories in this book have been a wake up call!

Please log on to www.teenagebluez.lifechangingbooks.net to vote for your favorite story. Also, send us a message on our Message Board. We really want to hear your opinions of our stories.

CALL FOR
<u>STORY SUBMISSIONS</u>

We're now accepting all ideas/submissions for short stories to be included in Teenage Bluez – Series #3. All submissions must be at least 20 pages, but no longer than 30 pages. Stories submitted must not contain any profanity or explicit sex scenes. Teenage male authors are welcome. All submissions must deal with today's teenage issues, such as, but not limited to: Peer Pressure, Drugs, Parents and Teen Relationships.

Submit all stories to:
www.teenagebluez.lifechangingbooks.net

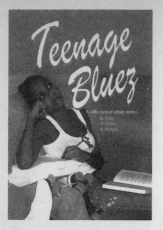 

$10.99

Maryland residents, please add 5% sales tax.
+ Shipping/handling$3.50 (U.S. Priority Mail)

Make check or money order payable to:
Life Changing Books
(please do not send cash)

Life Changing Books
PO Box 423, Brandywine, MD 20613

Purchaser information: (please print)

Name_____

Address_____

City_____

State and Zip_____

Number of books requested   _____

Total for this order $_____

Additional copies may also be ordered online at

TEENAGE BLUEZ SERIES #3

COMING SOON!!!!

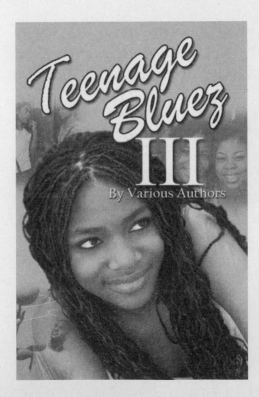

MEMBER OF SCABRINI GROUP

Québec, Canada
2006